I0737938

UNSAFE UNSCARED

◆◆◆

AVERY MOORE

ISBN: 978-1-7332861-0-7 (Paperback)
ISBN: 978-1-7332861-1-4 (ebook)
ISBN: 978-1-7332861-2-1 (audiobook)

Cover design by Nye' Lyn Tho
Cover photography by Avery Moore
Cover models: Lorenzo Martinez and Maurice Chapman
Book design by Avery Moore

Printed by IngramSpark in the United States of America

First printing edition 2020.

Ego Suicide
P.O. Box 7147
Oakland, CA 94601

UnsafeUnscared.com

Chapter 1 – Flashback 1999, Marcus

"What do you want?" my big brother asked, staring ahead, as we walked up to the gas station. Quintavious was eleven and I was nine. He was big, looked about thirteen, and was about his business. His legs moved so fast I had to skip and shuffle to keep up.

"Starburst," I said. Then I thought about how Starbursts aren't that big. *"No, Mambas."*

"If you don't make up your mind I ain't getting you nothing. You can't be taking forever to decide on something. You gotta be on point. You gotta be smooth."

"I am smooth—you just don't let me do nothing."

"You not ready. You too little, that's why," Quint said.

"No I ain't—I could do it this time—I even got pockets," I said, and pulled my tiny empty pockets out of my shorts.

"You ain't doing nothing—go over to the sodas and act like you gon buy something."

He never let me steal stuff. And it wasn't because I was scared. My friend Reggie was only six and he already stole something. Maybe I was a little bit scared. The man in there was mean and if he got you he would call the police on you—even if you were just a kid.

We walked in and I went up to the sodas like Quint said. I stood there looking at them. Then another group of kids came inside and went over to the candy. I was looking at them and trying to figure out if they were going to buy something or steal something, but then they got so quiet that you could tell they were going to steal.

I waited, trying to act regular—I felt like there was a spotlight shining down on me. And I wasn't even the one doing something wrong. All I had to do was look at the sodas. I kept looking. I opened the glass door and then shut it again. The cold air felt good. I wanted to look over and see how Quint was doing but I knew I shouldn't. I had to be smooth.

Then I heard the gas station man talking to someone at the counter. I looked up and saw that it was a policeman. Dang... I tried not to breathe too loud. The policeman kept walking and came right over next to me. He smiled at me and pulled a Mountain Dew from the cooler. I'll never forget that smile. Those purple lips and them big teeth. All my nightmares would have the same purple lips and them same big teeth show up for a long, long time.

Some of the kids started leaving the store. I could see Quint going to the door too. Then the man talked to the policeman loud enough for everyone to hear. "There's kids stealing, every day, from my store."

Quint heard him too, and then for some reason he took off running through the door.

"He's stealing right now! He's stealing right now!" The man spun around the counter, knocking over the display of Slim Jims and scattering them onto the floor. The policeman bolted after both of them, running and yelling into his walkie-talkie at the same time.

I started running too, trying to catch up. The gas station man turned around and went back to the store almost right away—so then it was just three of us. My brother was a block in front of me and the police was halfway between us. He yelled at Quint to stop but Quint kept going down Juniper Street. I could tell he was going to the house and I knew he was gonna take the cut by Ms. Lewis's house because that's the fastest way.

He did. The cop was mobbing after him, catching up. My brother was always big, so even though he was running his fastest, he wasn't going that fast. The cop wasn't very fast either though. I could almost catch up with both of them, and I was only nine.

Quint made it to the end of the cut and went left on 82nd—our block. It was only a little bit more to our house. He was going to make it! Maybe he could sneak into the backyard and hide.

I saw the cop turn left and when I finally got through the cut, I saw Quint running to our front yard. Then I noticed that Daddy was outside mowing the lawn.

Quint went straight for the gate on the side of the house, but it was padlocked like always. He started climbing. The police ran to the yard. I'm watching Quint climb that gate. I'm watching my dad watch the policeman. Then I'm watching the policeman; he stops in the middle of the front yard and pulls out his taser. I knew what a taser looked like but everything was going so fast that I didn't know if it was a taser or a pistol *he was aiming at Quint. He stopped, put his legs wide, and then blasted my brother. He blasted my brother off the gate and onto the ground.*

I stopped running.

I saw my dad.

I saw my dad charging toward the man. The man began to turn, but my dad was going full speed. Nothing could have stopped my dad. It was like he was playing football—the way his shoulder and head slammed into the man's chest. Like a safety taking out a wide receiver coming across the middle. The taser and the man's sun glasses went airborne.

My dad was on top of the man and boxed him with two blows to the face. There were sirens. The man reached for his pistol and my dad knocked him some more. There were tires skidding. My dad used his legs to keep the man pinned down.

Then there were police coming out of their cars. They yelled at my dad. My dad put his hands in the air. And then the cop on the ground shouted from the bottom of his chest: "FIIIIIIRE!"

All I heard were blasts and blasts and blasts. They weren't tasers. They fired and fired and fired on my dad. Into his chest and his shoulders. They fired into him until he was dead.

I saw that.

Chapter 2 – 2009, Quintavious

It's about that time of night—he won't be hitting nothing and he just needs to accept it.

Oh well. Quintavious tosses the near-empty 211 can at the dumpster. The Steel Reserve—that potent malt liquor that gets you there quick. It was about his eighth or ninth tall one of the night— he can't quite remember—but by now he's good and confident, warm and comfortable.

He's walking home but he's not ready to go home—he needs something to happen. It's too fucking boring. He needs action.

Something that reminds him he's alive. That breaks him out of his head. He thirsts for it. A climax—that is what he needs. Sex would do. A fight would do.

He searches his surroundings—nothing but snow-covered streets and storefronts. It's 3:30 a.m. and there's not a person in sight. Fuck.

He walks on, yearning for somebody, anybody. Even a knock or a homeless guy—they could ask him for a cigarette and he could say no, have a conversation—can he at least get that? Fuck, man, something's got to give—it's like there's a mosquito perched on his brain that needs to be slapped.

He remembers the blunt roach he saved and steers his big body towards shelter on the side of Popeye's. He looks at his reflection and laughs at himself for wearing such old clothes—his Braves Starter jacket over a dark blue hoodie, black jeans, and black J's. He wears these clothes when his others are dirty, but there's a reason he's kept them this long—they're his favorites. He's always loved the jacket, the hoodie went with it, and the jeans just fit his legs for some reason.

He reaches in the pocket of his hoodie and pulls out the cellophane cigarette wrapper that protects the blunt. He fingers around his pockets for a lighter and comes up with two. It makes him feel a little better—he loves it when that happens. He lifts the lighter to his teeth, fits his unusually long canine into the thin metal child safety band and pops it into his mouth with one quick pry. He spits it to the ground like a sunflower seed.

As he torches the tip of the roach, he appreciates the fact that he didn't smoke it with the homies earlier in the night. The cherry glows as he inhales. He brings the hit into his chest. His inhale is fast and strong until the heat scratches the back of his throat; then he takes the blunt from his lips and sucks in the icy air. He feels it push the smoke down to his belly. The herb creeps into his head and he feels his brain swell. Suddenly the cold night changes from something he battles to something that is home—from his enemy to a beautiful photograph he's exploring. He listens to his footsteps in the snow—the crushing of tiny chunks of ice. The rhythm of his feet sway him into a meditation. Kshshshsh, kshshshsh, kshshshshsh…

He zones into his walk for one, two, three blocks.

His trance is broken by a strange noise—a human sound. A heave… A cough… Quint follows the noise until he sees the source. It's a white college girl on her hands and knees, vomiting onto the asphalt in the parking lot next to a small playground. This is the spot for college parties—he's been to a couple at the apartments across the street.

He watches her stomach clench every few seconds and squeeze out yellowy bile. She relaxes and rests her head on the concrete bar at the end of a parking space that shows cars they've gone too far. She isn't aware that he's there; he feels like he's watching a movie. Why isn't anybody out here helping her? "You all right?" he breaks the silence, but there's no response. He says it again.

"It's perfectly… it's perfectly… fine," she says, and looks up at him. She stares for a few seconds, like a dog momentarily looking up from its dog food. He looks back at her face, trying to think about who she looks like. She favors someone, but who is it? Oh, it's the dark haired chick from Friends, that's who it is.

He's happy that she's not running away—scared of a black man, or any man, walking up to her at four in the morning. Instead, she's acting like she was expecting him to be there. "It was a mixture of tequilaaaaaa, and gin, I think... I'm never drinking again," she says. Quint laughs. He's said that same shit before—multiple times.

He stands over her, watching. He likes the way she looks. Like a picture. Not sexually. White girls are just too different. Especially college white girls. It's not comfortable. It's not the same. He'll do it. Don't get him wrong—he's not going to pass it up, but it's not the same. It's too much drama, and he doesn't like sex when they're fucking him because he's black and he's fucking them because they're white—like to try someone from the other side. All that crazy fetish-type stuff is for the birds—he's old school. But look at her—she's beautiful—not sexually, but just like when you can tell an auntie or a cousin is attractive.

Her head tilts up to his and her dark eyes follow; a guilty smile tightens her lips. Her face is sweaty and her little body quivers in the wind. Quint squats down to her level. "Your friends leave you?" He thought girls covered each other's backs in these situations.

"Well, they've been problematic before," she says. "My so-called friends have been the ones to do this time and time again. But you cannot blame them—they're just a product of the messed up system." All right, she's drunk. Because *he's* drunk, and he still knows that *that* didn't make no sense. "But, I see now, they are not here... It's just you... Oh well... You know who you do resemble quite a bit though? Rrrrrrrobert Kelly."

"Robert Kelly?"

"Robert Kelly," she says, and spits. "Rhythm and Blues singer. Pop sensation," she mutters.

"Oh, you talking about R. Kelly! That's funny—I don't look nothing like that man. I'm about twice R. Kelly's size." He stands and leans back on his straightened left leg.

"Anyhow," she says, then closes her eyes, takes a deep breath and blows out a long exhale like she's in a yoga class. "What's over is over. The rest is up to me." Whatever she means by that, Quint can tell she's irritated.

She spits into her pile a couple of times, then scrunches her face and blows out her nose. Nothing much comes out, so she squeezes the bridge of her nose with her thumb and pointer and slides her fingers off the tip. She flicks her hand toward the ground like there's a spider on it, sending a mixture of snot and throw-up deep into the bed of snow. If a guy was doing this, Q probably wouldn't even have noticed. And if he was sober and saw a girl doing it, he'd probably think it was nasty. But right now it's just making him laugh.

"Sexy, huh?" she says, looking up at him with sweaty hair and lively eyes.

"I guess… But I'll tell you what you *should* do is drink some water," he says with glazed and squinted eyes.

"Yeah, yeah, yeah, that's what they all say. An urban myth," she answers.

"No. I think that shit is true," Quint says.

He watches her wipe her hands on a clean patch of snow, get up and walk back to the apartment. Damn, he wonders what her name is.

"Ramona!" she says, like she was reading his mind, and then mumbles, "That's my name," as she hits the buzzer. A few seconds later the intercom blasts unintelligible drunken white yells before buzzing her in. Quint considers going up there with her—and knows that he would have, too, if he hadn't smoked already. He would have at least walked through and seen what's up with the ladies and free beer. Try to have some of that sex he doesn't like having. But he doesn't feel like it now. He's calm. He's chill. He stands still for a few seconds, thinking about her as he looks at the pile of vomit that's turning snow into steam, and then starts walking.

Will she recognize him if he runs into her again, or even remember that this happened? She could black it all out. There've been times when he didn't remember whole chunks of the night. Nights when somebody'd tell him something he did and he'd be like, "Damn, for real?" He remembers one night, Marcus and T boxed each other and in the morning neither of them remembered, so he just told them the bruises must have been from the snowball fight they had. But does it still affect you? Like if he didn't remember and she didn't remember, would it have any effect on you at all? Why is he even thinking about this? Damn he must be high.

The walk home goes by like nothing. The coldness feels fine and the minutes go quick. He wonders if he'll ever see her again. He should've got her number. No, that's not right—she was throwing up in the snow. You can't do that. At least he knows her name. Ramona. Ramona.

He gets to his apartment. His body feels worn out but his mind feels wide awake. And it's a good thing, too, because Marcus's punk

ass took the key from the hiding place under the plant! It's not the first time this has happened, though, so he knows the drill.

Quint goes around to the front of the building and faces Marcus's bedroom window. He takes a piss at the base of a tree and watches the snow melt—it reminds him of her.

Okay, enough playing around, time to get down to business. He scoops up some snow, packs it into the size of a baseball, and takes a few steps closer to the building. He calculates the angle carefully because the snowball needs to hit the window hard enough to wake him up but not so hard that it wakes up every tenant in the building. Especially Tony's grandma, Ms. Morgan. She will curse you out *and* call your mama.

Quint aims and throws… No sign. He tosses a few more off Marcus's window… Still no sign. He steps back and packs two hard ones. He fires the first one and waits… no signal. Fuck it. Marcus leaves him no choice—he winds up and delivers a rocket to the dead center of the window. Blam! It vibrates. Quint jumps behind a car to hide from whoever woke up. His brother was probably in a deep dream, but if the first few throws appear in his dream like flicks to the ear, this one is a two-by-four to the head.

The bedroom light flashes on and off a few times—their signal for success. Then Quint notices Ms. Morgan's light is on too. He peeks above the hood of the car to see her putting on her bifocals and scanning the street for hoodlums. Good thing she can't see too well.

Quint sneaks to the door and Marcus lets him in. He's home free. Even his mom doesn't seem to wake up as he comes in. But then again, you never know with her—she might get on him about it in the morning.

He goes to the bathroom, drinks some water hand-to-mouth, pats the dogs on the head, strips down his layers onto the floor and flops into bed. His mind is happy as he slips into sleep.

Chapter 3 – Flashback 1999, Nick

Mama and Alex were standing and blocking the TV so I squeezed through, and I saw police lights on the screen and then Dad. Dad in his police suit and he was on TV.

"Mom, what? What Mom? What happened to Dad?" Alex said—he was eleven and I was nine.

"Shshsht," Mom said. "Daddy's okay."

Then she said a guy got dead, but not Dad—a bad guy or something. So we went to the hospital because Dad had a scratch or a bump. But he didn't get dead—they just made him go to the hospital because.

It took like forty million hours to get there. But it was worth it—dad was on TV! And when we got there he wasn't dead. He was in there in a hospital costume with all his police friends. The only thing that really looked weird was his eye was closed; it was squeezed closed, so it looked like he was always closing his eye.

"There's my old lady and the boys," Dad yelled. "Thought they were gonna leave me here!"

"Can ya blame 'em?" a different guy said.

Mama had Dad's clothes and then he put them on in the bathroom. Then we started to go, but we didn't know how to get out. Dad said he knew the way and then Mama said she knew the way and then no one knew the way so we just kept walking around in the hospital for ever. I didn't care though because my Dad was on TV – he was a hero. He had a fight with a bad guy and the bad guy got dead.

We were walking for so long, and then the thing happened with the lady.

The lady stopped and pointed at us—she was brown and had a wet face from crying. She pointed at us and then her face changed slowly like she was going to explode. Then she screamed. It was like a million alarms going off at the same time. And her body looked like five million bees were stinging her. You couldn't hear anything else. My dad pushed my head around and made us go the other way, but she still screamed and looked at Dad, and then she followed us. All the other people around stopped and looked at her and looked at us. We were walking, but nobody else was walking—they were just standing there. And then she stopped screaming and everything was like frozen except for us, because we were the only ones walking. Dad grabbed my arm and pulled me to go faster—he wanted to get away. But when we almost got away and couldn't see her anymore, that's when she really really really really screamed—I covered my ears because it was like my head was stuck in a fire engine.

"You killed my husband!" she said. "You killed my husband! You killed my husband!" And then she just fell down because she was so sad.

And then she said, "You killed Bobby."

And she was saying Dad did it.

Chapter 4 — 2009, Nick

Nick throws the sponge into the sink and goes to get his jacket. "Did you wipe the counters?" his mom yells from the other room.

Jesus—you give her an inch and she asks for a mile. Nick frantically sweeps the sponge across the tile, with half the particles going in his cupped hand and half on the floor. "What was Dad doing here this morning? Alex said he came by in his fucking uniform and car and everything."

"He has a new beat and so he said he's coming by to check in on you boys," his mom says.

"Good job, Dad. Check on your kids. Too bad you're like fifteen years late and they're all grown up, Dumbass."

"Nick. Watch your language."

"What, you don't think Dad's a dumbass?"

"Cut it out," she says. "Oh, he also wants to come by your new job to get a banner made for the police barbecue. I told him to talk to you."

"How does he even know where I work? He's not coming to my job. Fucking stalker." Nick opens the cupboard and takes a five stack of OREO's. "Seriously—you fucked up raising your kids. It's okay. Get over it. I don't want your last name. I don't want you stopping by. If you want to give me some cash, yes I'll take it," Nick says. He looks at the oven clock and sees that it's past nine, so he hurries down the hall to his older brother's room to get the whiskey he stashed under the bed. Alex is huddled in the corner listening to sports talk radio and cutting out collages from magazines. He's probably starting a manic episode. Nick checks again to see if Alex wants to come out with him, but he doesn't, which is probably better. "All right, I love you bro," he says.

His mom reminds him that they're having family over tomorrow for Whitney's graduation party. "Okay," Nick says. He leaves the house and climbs into his little blue pickup. Finally! Fuckin' A. He knew he should have just gone to Taco Bell. Oh well. Within ten seconds, the ignition is on and Nick has shifted from first to second to third gear. The needle on the tachometer goes back and forth like windshield wipers as he bounces up the block and then jerks to a halt at the stop sign. They did a good job salting the streets tonight—no black ice.

It only takes him seven minutes to get to Ronald's apartment. He circles the block once and then sees a space—right on the other side of the intersection. Fuck yeah. A green Saturn is the only car in front of him. "Bro, you take my spot, you sign your death warrant," Nick threatens into his dashboard. The man drives past the space, so Nick zooms straight into it. He cuts off the ignition and looks up to see the Saturn stationary with its blinker on. Nick opens his door and sees the dude's window rolling down.

"Excuse me, sir, I was waiting to park there," the guy says.

"This isn't a parallel parking spot, bro," Nick says.

"I had my blinker on, that's why," he says in a polite Latino accent with a slight lisp to it.

"Sorry, man, if you saw the spot, you would be in here, but you passed it up."

"Sir, with all due respect, there's more than one way to park. I had my blinker on," the guy says. Nick picks up his bottle of liquor and locks the doors. This guy is off his rocker. Maybe it's better to just give him the spot—if the dude really wants it that bad. Nick turns, but before he can speak, the man says, "Fuck you then cracker! Let me see you out again. You better watch your truck—I'll slit your tires." He peels out.

Nick feels his heart beating as he walks away. He keeps his neck locked, face forward, as his stilt legs march down the block and up to Ronald's apartment.

The door's unlocked so he lets himself in. Ronald and Scriv are watching ESPN on mute, listening to Akon and, what a surprise, arguing:

"So you're saying you want a girlfriend who everyone *wants* to fuck, but who nobody *thinks* about fucking?" Scriv says.

"I want to be attracted to my girlfriend—I don't care if other people think she's attractive or not."

"Exactly," Scriv says, reclined, with red eyes. "You can't control if other people find her attractive. And you can't control if they jack off to her. It's just the way it is, bro. It's life. Just consider it a compliment."

"You know what else is life? Me kicking someone's ass if I catch them jacking off to my girlfriend," Ronald says.

"How could you *catch* someone jacking off to your girl-friend—you can't see what people are thinking," Scriv says.

"Can you two jackasses shut the fuck up?" Nick interjects. "And Ron—don't you think you need to do one thing at a time? Like, get a girlfriend, before you start trying to protect her from people's thoughts?"

Nick reveals the plastic bottle of Ancient Age whiskey to the fellas and gets several claps from Ronald and a smile from Scriv. "Clapping is great and all, but you owe me some money," Nick says.

"Put it on my tab," Ronald says. These bastards never pay. Nick takes a swig of liquor and passes it on.

"Bro—listen to what happened to me on my way here," Nick says. "So I'm going past the intersection and I see a parking spot, right? It's the first one past the light so I just drive right into it. So this guy is one car in front of me and he stops his car, puts on his blinker and tries to act like he needs to back into my spot, but I'm already parked there. I get out of the truck and smile right in his face. 'Excuse me, sir, I was going to park here first,' he says, right? I tell the guy he has two choices—he can pay me a hundred dollars and I'll consider letting his ass have the spot, or he can kiss my white ass, play by the rules, and find his own fucking spot… Let's just say he chose option B." Ronald and Scriv chuckle, like they're hearing a story that they've heard before. They pass the bottle a few more rounds.

Time for a cigarette.

Nick walks to the steps to smoke. He sees Damon coming up, his daddy-long-legs taking four stairs at a time. They meet at the small balcony and, like it's been since seventh grade, Nick feels like a small child next to Damon's six foot five frame. They slap hands and Nick asks him what's going on.

"Yep, dude, I quit smoking," he says.

"Right on, bro, congratulations," Nick says, peeling the gold plastic strip off a fresh pack of Dorals.

"Yeah. Right now I only smoke when I drink," he says.

"You mind if I have one in front of you?"

"Go for it," Damon says, clutching both hands on the top of the short, cast iron railing and leaning down and back, like a water skier holding onto a rope, somehow stretching his back. "I'll have one too since I'll be drinking later on," he says.

They smoke in silence for a minute. It's always calm and re-laxed when chilling with Damon. No pressure to talk. No pressure to be quiet. That's just the kind of guy he is.

The smooth drags on the cigarette activates the buzz from the whiskey and Nick sinks into the comfort of the moment. His skin goes numb—he'll be ready to hit the bars soon.

"Did you end up calling that girl?" Damon says.

"Bro… Tried calling her yesterday." Nick stands up and gets in his story-telling position—less than two feet from Damon. "She picks up, right?" Damon doesn't say anything. "Keep in mind this is the same chick that was hanging on me over at Frazier's. The same chick that took *my* phone from *my* hand and put *her* number in it." He looks at Damon. Damon nods. "So she picks up. I tell her it's Nick… 'Nick who?' she says." Damon shakes his head. "After she said that, I knew it wasn't gonna work out. I told her 'how many fucking Nicks do you give your number to?' She said she was busy but she'll call me back." Nick looks at Damon, who doesn't say anything. "She didn't call me back, bro. I'm done getting numbers—I swear—I'm not even gonna ask anymore."

"Yeah," Damon says.

"I went home with a big girl the other night though. That was fun. I'm telling you, titties flying everywhere," Nick says.

Damon chuckles and spits off the balcony. "Damn, dude, with your skinny ass? What'd that look like, a ham hock and a toothpick?"

"You love picturing me naked, don't you?" Nick says.

They finish their cigarettes and join Ronald and Scriv. The four of them drink the rest of the Ancient Age and get into Damon's Ford Taurus. They drive up to the east side of the lake toward the bars.

Nick's fade is on as he walks into Frazier's. His head is straight. One of the songs end but his swagger is unstoppable on his way into the restroom. He bobs over to the urinal and undoes his belt to take a piss. As he pees, he feels his phone vibrate. It's probably what's-her-name calling back. He reaches down with his left hand. FUCK! His phone's not vibrating at all… he's just peeing on the tip of his belt! He moves the leather out of the line of fire and sees urine concentrated on the crotch and right thigh area of his jeans, so he takes some water from the tap and splashes it onto himself in random areas to create the spilt-water-and-not-piss look. He washes his hands, douses his pale white face, runs his fingers over his nearly shaved head, then rubs the water off his face with the inside of his shoulder. Good to go.

Next stop, the bar.

"How much for a whiskey and coke?" Nick asks, trying to stick with the same liquor—less chance of a hangover.

"Five."

"How about a Long Island?"

"Same."

"I'll take the Long Island." There's a right price for everything. "And a water for my girlfriend," he adds.

"Bottle or tap?"

"Tap," Nick says.

The eighty year-old sitting on the stool next to him shakes his head. "There's two things I'll never pay for," he says. "Pussy and water."

"No shit." Nick drops six dollars on the counter, grabs his drinks and walks toward the crowd. He scans the scene for hotties without boyfriends—looks like there's a couple. There's definitely one sitting with her friend at a high table on the right of the dance floor. Money—he goes over and says what's up.

"Notheeeeeeen," she says, avoiding eye contact and holding her breath like she just found a fly in her salad.

"Do you go to the university?" Nick asks. "You look so famil-iar."

"Noooooooooo?" she says, still looking totally grossed out.

The other girl tilts her head. "Um, no offense, but actually my friend doesn't really feel like talking to you."

"Oh, are you her personal talker? Her assistant? She's not at the point where she can talk to people in the bar by herself yet?" Nick says.

"Can you just, like, leave us alone?"

"It's called having a conversation—that's what you do at a bar. I wasn't trying to hit on you—trust me—don't flatter yourself," Nick says. He retreats, trying to shake it off. What are they even doing here? Why did they come? Like if they really wanted to drink water and talk about their periods, why didn't they go to Starbucks?

Nick spots Ronald and Damon on the sidelines. He joins their conversation, but after three sentences he's distracted by the most beautiful woman he's ever seen. Soft, dark hair. Smooth, white skin—her face and lips so kissable. A nose ring. She's wearing a black and white striped top. But it's not just her look—you can see her personality. She's feisty, she loves to have fun. She would make a great mother. Smart, responsible. He can even picture the future—he sees her reading stories to the kids. "I'll be back," he says to Damon and moves in her direction.

He hesitates, not really feeling like the man after that last interaction. One more drink, that'll help. He dips his hands into both pockets, feeling for anything resembling a bill. Keys, cigarettes, wallet, ear buds, pencil, lighter, toothpicks, mints, and then, maybe... it feels thin and papery... he lifts it out... a receipt. Son of a bitch. Plan B. He starts walking the perimeter of the club, weaving through groups of people who come together and actually sit together... Squares. His eyes continue surveying until he zeroes in on a half full tap beer. The beer's owner is in deep conversation a few feet away, so Nick walks up naturally and takes the beer, like it's his, and then walks off like the whole club is his.

Now he's ready. This could be the most important night of his life. The night he meets his wife. The story of their first encounter will get told again and again.

As he pushes himself through the thick crowd, his attention is caught by a freshly cracked Corona. It stands alone on a tall round table, like in a beer commercial. No one's in sight. Some dude probably bought it for some chick and she didn't feel like drinking it. He grabs it and returns to Ronald to give him the tap beer.

"Right on," says Ronald.

"Bro, I took this Corona right in front of some dude with his girlfriend sitting right there. He said, 'Hey, man, that's my beer.' I said, 'really, bro? What's your name? Because unless your name is Corona—in which case your name is on this beer—then guess what, this is my fucking beer.' He just sat there, bro, I swear."

"I love you, bro," Ronald says, squinting his eyes at Nick.

"Serious as a heart attack," Nick mumbles. He pours the Corona into his mouth, thinking about the nose ring dream girl twenty feet away. Man, they would have the best sex ever. Wake up in the morning, smiling and laughing. What would their kids look like?"

"Dude!" Ronald says.   "Answer my question."

"Huh?"

"Forget about it. Who are you staring at?" Ronald asks. Nick tells him about the girl in the stripes.

"Yeah, I peeped her. Ask her if she can hook me up with a gift card at Foot Locker."

"Bro. Cool it. I could seriously settle down with that girl. No joke."

"Bro. Really, bro?"

"This is different."

"Oh, it's different? So this time you're going to actually talk to her? You need me to hold your hand?"

"I'll give you something to hold," Nick says. Ronald's right, though. It's time to hurry up—there's no telling where she'll be in fifteen minutes. Nick starts over and then fucking Beanie from high school bumps into him.

"Ni-i-i-i-i-ck Edwa-a-a-a-a-rds," Beanie says, sounding like a sheep and a frat boy at the same time.

"I switched my name, bro. I'm Nick Nelson now."

"Nick Nelson now! You got married?"

"Fuck you bro—I got rid of my dad's name. Bastard wasn't there, so why would I keep his name?"

"Ri-i-i-i-ght," Beanie says, and then goes on about "chasing wool" like he's still in high school.

"You're a dirty motherfucker, you know that?" Nick says. And it's true. Beanie is a dog—always has been. And the messed up part is girls still like him for some reason. When he was in high school, he got more blowjobs than anyone, and it was because he had a strategy. 'Go ahead,' he would say, 'just touch it, it's okay.' Then after touch it, it was, 'it's okay, just hold it.' After hold it, 'just give it a kiss.' He would keep going like that, and it worked.

Beanie's friend comes from the bar with shots of tequila. He sees Nick and shouts at the bartender to pour another. Nick takes the shot glass. A small voice tells him he shouldn't drink it. Then an enormous voice tells him that you can't turn down a drink, it's

Chapter 5 – Marcus

"Fuck them, Charles. Yeah I rather play my game than go try to suck some rich dick and get treated like a nigger," says Marcus as he plays Madden '08. "Look at me—do I look like a bitch nigga? Is that what I look like? 'Cause I ain't never been a bitch-made nigga; I ain't never been a sellout."

"First of all, stop cussing in the house. Your mama could be coming through that door any minute," says Charles, Marcus's mom's boyfriend, from the kitchen. Charles has been around for a while now, and he looooves to try to drop knowledge. "Second of the tray and slides it under the security window. The woman puts his Spicier Nacho chips and a Swisher in the tray and slides it back with some of his change still in it.

"Are we walking or driving?" Ronald says.

"Walking," says Damon.

"Driving," says Nick.

"I already have a DUI; we're walking," says Damon.

"Dog!" Nick says, and then walks into the middle of the street and stops. He spreads his arms out wide like he's stopping traffic. "Who *doesn't* have a DUI? Having a DUI is the same as jerking off—you ask ten guys if they have a DUI, nine are gonna say yeah and the last one is a liar!"

"You wanna drive my car then?" Damon asks.

"Fuck yeah, I'll drive your car."

"Fuck you, bro, you're not driving my car."

They walk to Ron's.

Chapter 5 – Marcus

"Fuck them, Charles. Yeah I rather play my game than go try to suck some rich dick and get treated like a nigger," says Marcus as he plays Madden '08. "Look at me—do I look like a bitch nigga? Is that what I look like? 'Cause I ain't never been a bitch-made nigga; I ain't never been a sellout."

"First of all, stop cussing in the house. Your mama could be coming through that door any minute," says Charles, Marcus's mom's boyfriend, from the kitchen. Charles has been around for a while now, and he looooves to try to drop knowledge. "Second of all," he continues, "since when is getting a job sucking dick? I always thought men got jobs so they have some paper so they can take a girl out so they can *get* they dick sucked…" Charles washes his face and cracks a cold one.

"That's how it be though,"— more quietly so his mom won't hear if she walks in. "It's set up against us. You know what they say, right—crackers don't buy slaves no more, they rent them," Marcus says, leaning with his joystick. "Naw, but for real, don't nobody want to hire me anyways," he says, lying on the carpet with a bean bag chair propping his head up.

Charles looks down at Marcus— the light from the TV bouncing on and off his face. He takes a drink of his Natural Light. "That's the problem with youngsters these days—they want money, but they don't want to work," Charles says. "At the end of the day, you're either gonna be broke on the street, or in a house with some money in your pocket—money that you got from a job. I know you think you gonna be a little rapper but guess what, that shit ain't happening."

"Okay," Marcus says quietly, nodding his head. "Watch."

"And especially if you ain't got no job? How you gonna record something if you ain't got no money for studio time? What you gonna do, trap?" Charles pauses. "I'm not worried about that. That won't never happen. I know that. You not gonna risk jail time so you can turn more of these youngsters out here into knocks…"

"Oh my God, here you go with your long-old lectures again— I told you you shoulda been a teacher with all them lectures you be havin," Marcus says as he runs a Halfback Slant.

Charles ignores him. "Imagine you causing one of your friends to become a crackhead like what's-his-name that damn near got shot trying to steal them chairs off the balcony. Like your uncle—after all your momma done for him, he gon steal her checkbook? And when you gave him that two dollars and he ain't ate nothing in a week, he still gonna go out and buy him another rock?" Charles says.

"You can't blame it on the supplier—they still make the choice to smoke that shit. And when you really think about it, the CIA is the one that really brought that shit in here in the first place."

"See, you blame blame blame blame blame."

"It's true though!"

"It don't matter if it's true! You gonna be sitting in a motherfucking prison cell blaming this person, that person, the government, the police. But guess what? Even if you right. Even if it is they fault, you think they gonna let you out? Huh? You think they gonna be like 'Oh, you right. You right, it is they fault. It is the white man's fault. Here you go, you're free.' Huh? They gonna say that...? No! You *still* gonna be sitting in that prison cell. You need to stop blaming everybody and start doing what you can do to help your life."

"We need more people saying fuck this shit, that's what we need. We got too many motherfuckers playing into the system, and that's the problem," Marcus says.

"How many people make it ten years hustling without ending up dead or in prison? One out of ten?"

"One out of four."

"I don't think so, but even if that's true, one out of four? You want to gamble your life, your freedom, for a one out of four chance? That's some bad odds. I remember it took me one time to get locked up to realize okay, this ain't for me. I must not be a very good criminal if I'm getting locked up."

"You stupid," Marcus smiles and shakes his head.

"And then these youngsters that risking lockup to be a runner for somebody?" Charles continues. "To run they ass down across town in the middle of winter to deliver a dime bag and get kicked two dollars? You gotta be kidding me—you won't even run to the corner store to get some milk, so what the fuck you wanna do that for, to *keep it real*? I was born at night, I wasn't born last night."

"You got me fucked up. Now you talking to me like I'm thirteen years old. And another thing, I don't have anything serious on my record, so really, you need to be giving this lecture to somebody else," Marcus says.

"That's the reason I'm giving it to you. You don't have a record so why would you risk lock up to do something like that when you could be coolin inside with central heat and air making eight dollars a hour. These little niggas out here don't make forty dollars a day. Not the ones starting out. Maybe on they best day, but not every day."

"You acting like everybody could just get a job—like it's just jobs waiting on people," Marcus says.

"You could get a job if you really wanted it. But I'm not gonna tell you nothing that you already know. Just 'cause you ain't working for the Black Panthers don't mean you selling out. You gotta start at the bottom like everybody else. When we was young we took any job we could get. We appreciated that shit. I don't know why you scared to work at the sign shop—I told you I most likely be able to get you a job there—you just have to go get a interview with Gary—he'll give you a chance."

"I'll think about it."

"And if you don't want to work for nobody, then work for yourself."

Marcus pauses his game and perks his head up. "What are you talking about?"

"You know what I'm talking about. It's the middle of winter. Go get you a shovel and start knocking on doors," Charles says.

Marcus unpauses the game. "Got me fucked up… too cold for all that."

"Yep, got an excuse for everything," Charles says, walking past Marcus to the bathroom. "And if you don't stop taking my socks! You already made me write my name on them, and you still wearing them!"

Marcus looks down on his feet and notices the Cs on the toes of his socks. "My fault," he smiles and keeps playing his x-box. "But hey, I'm about to go to the studio in a minute and lay down some hits—right when I get done with this game."

"Okay, I believe it when I see it. You probably be playing that game till dark. I never understood why you like playing that so much anyway."

Marcus gets an interception and leans with the controller as he breaks tackles for twenty yards. "Same reason I like pussy, my nigga—it keeps me occupied."

Chapter 6 – Nick

Nick wakes up on the floor of Ronald's living room with his head one inch from the TV that's blasting a re-run of Blind Date. He looks up and surveys his surroundings: Ronald's on the couch in a sleeping bag and Damon's standing up in the middle of the room rocking back and forth and eating toast.

"What's up, pimp?" Ronald says. Nick just looks at him and says what's up with his head. He rotates around and grabs a pillow from the floor near the wall so he can watch the TV and not just hear it banging into his head like a fire drill. He feels hungover so he goes into the bathroom and starts taking a shit, but then the smell makes him want to throw up so he flips around and throws up into the toilet, then sits back down, finishes his business and flushes. He washes his hands and face, cups his hands to drink some water, finds a bottle of Motrin on the floor, takes a few of those, and walks back into the room.

"You still have that wet weed?" Nick says, and for some reason they all start laughing.

"The bowl's over there, spark it up," Damon says. Nick goes over to get it and it's sitting next to some crusty nuggets and a few seeds. He smokes the rest of the bowl that was already in there and then packs another and passes it around. Sometimes smoking helps his hangover.

"You got any food?" Nick asks.

"Bread, no butter. Got some mayonnaise."

"I'm all right. I need to get going anyway."

"Dude, you don't need to pretend. Everybody knows you don't have shit to do today."

"It's my cousin's graduation and my mom is having the party."

"Little Whitney's done with high school? She's eighteen already? Let me come to the party!"

"Fifth grade graduation, dumbass—you fucking pedophile."

"My bad, dude. Why are you guys having a graduation party for fifth grade? My mom barely came to my high school graduation," Ronald says.

"Yeah bro. That's the difference between me and you—we take school serious in my family," Nick says as he pulls on his socks and shoes.

"All right then man, we'll probably be over there in a minute—get some of your mom's food in my stomach."

"Yep," Damon adds.

"All right," Nick says and heads out to his truck, only to find a parking ticket on the windshield. Great, he doesn't fucking drink and drive and this is his reward. He gets in and drives home – half high, half hungover, and half pissed off about the ticket.

***

Nick goes into the living room and says hi to the graduate Whitney, to Aunt Leelee, and to Grampa. His lesbian aunt Leelee is drinking her favorite, tomato juice mixed with Budweiser, and talking with some relative who's cool but who Nick's too hungover to remember her name. "No, I'm not into straight girls. I know what you mean though, these tri-sexuals kissing each other in front of a bunch of boys. Oh, uh, uh," Aunt Leelee says.

"Tri-sexuals?" Nick asks.

"Yeah, tri-sexuals. These bitches'll try anything!" He walked right into that one.

"That's okay! Let them experiment if they want," Nick says.

"Whatever, you *would* say that," Aunt Leelee says. "So how was the breeder bar last night?"

"Lame," Nick says. "Not enough tri-sexuals." He goes to check on his grandpa. As always, he's wearing cowboy boots, blue jeans and a short-sleeved collared shirt with his Copenhagen can in the chest pocket.

Grampa's talking about how he got lost on the west side driving over here. "It was a colored lady that gave me directions. Boy was she nice. I tell ya. I got out of the truck. I said, 'Ma'am, I'm sorry to bother you. I'm a hick from the sticks, and I'm lost. And to be honest, I'm a little scared.' And she smiled and laughed and got me right back on my way. Boy was she nice…" Grampa says and then looks up to see Nick. "Alex," he says as Nick's walking over, "grab your old grampa a Pepsi, would ya?" He always mixes up the names of his grandchildren.

"You got it," Nick says, and goes in the fridge for a Pepsi. "I don't know who it was, but some jackass only got Coke."

"That's okay, I'm not thirsty anyhow. Thank you," he says. "So, you have fun last night?"

"Too much fun," Nick says, trying to point out the fact that he drank too much and feels like shit. Grampa thinks it means he got lucky.

"Nothing wrong with that. I'll tell ya something, Nicky." He gets a serious tone to his voice. "I think by now everyone in the family knows I'm not a religious-type person. Some people believe, and that's fine… Me, I don't. But I'll tell you, Nicky, if there is a God, and he made anything better than pussy, he must've kept it for himself," and they both start cracking up.

"You're right about that," Nick says. They talk about the price of cattle going down and Grampa tells him a couple stories about Gloria, his neighbor who just went to heaven, and then Nick gets some potato salad and a Sprite and goes back into the kitchen. He still feels under the weather and tells his mom he thinks he caught a bug.

"Yeah right, like the bug at the bottom of the tequila bottle?" She laughs at her own joke.

"It's a worm, Mom. Good try," he says, and then heads to the bathroom to throw up, but can't, so he goes back out. "I think I'm gonna head over to my place and spray down that couch I just got."
"You got a couch?"

"Yeah. I got a couch off this guy over by my apartment for twenty-five bucks. But the only problem is it has water damage on the bottom and I think there's bugs in it so I'm gonna spray it down."

"Honey you might need to bring it out in the sun for a while."

"Too cold for that."

"Well if it's at all sunny out, put it out on your balcony—because I don't know if spray will do anything. You could try it."

Nick drives home. He parks, walks upstairs to his apartment and goes inside. Fuck, there are five roaches running around like bumper cars on the floor of his kitchen. He gets his can of Raid and starts chasing them around, spraying the laser stream into whatever corner they sneak into. He gets two of them, watches them flip over and do their death dance, and then walks into his room and tips over onto the mattress. So much for getting anything done today. He lies there. He should get some water. But he can't. The smell of RAID is nauseating and he considers throwing up, but decides it would be better to just fall asleep. He can't though. He stares sideways. He's tired. He doesn't feel right. Nervousness. Disappointment. He stares at nothing in particular. He wishes people liked him more. Wishes he were better at things. That the girls liked him more. That would be nice. He wishes he had someone to come home to. This empty, dusty room with this mattress. What is the point of all this? It has to get better. He just needs to find the right girl. Maybe he should stop drinking so much.

He stares at the bottom of the window. He looks at the clock. He needs to move. He needs to turn on the TV. Where's the remote? It's probably on the floor. He can't bring himself to roll over to look for it. He just feels too tired. He flexes his arm into the bed to lift his body, and then collapses. He's too tired. He just needs to relax. A wave of something swirls through his body. He can't put a name on it. Nausea, anxiety, nerves. He's just paralyzed. His top and bottom teeth clench together. He wants to turn on the TV. To get distracted by something besides life. He starts at it again, but again buckles into his mattress, exhaling. He wants to look at the clock. The TV, actually. The TV would be better. Why can't he do anything right? What did he do last night? Fighting with some chick? What the fuck? What is *she* doing right now? Is she lying in bed, feeling like this?

Chapter 7 – Marcus

Marcus beats the Broncos with the Packers and then goes around the house looking for change. His mom doesn't care if he takes change from the kitchen or if he finds it around the house, just as long as he stays out of her purse. She will really kick him of the house if he takes even a quarter from her purse.

He counts two dollars and fifteen cents, which means he can take the train to the studio instead of walking. And it's a good thing because it's colder than a bitch and the studio is way down Patriot Blvd. As he enters the station, he sees that the lady isn't in her box, so he fronts like he's putting in a token and pulls the rotating bars of the turnstile inwards a half turn and then squeezes his stomach and slides past. Quint gets mad when he does this, but that's only because he's jealous that Marcus can fit through and his big ass can't. And it's a good strategy if you can fit because even if someone's looking over the surveillance camera they probably won't notice. And you better hope they don't, too, or else they'll lock you up for two weeks.

After waiting ten minutes, the Southbound train comes and Marcus walks on and takes a seat facing the lake. He rides around the west side of the lake where he lives, past the community college and the nice apartments, past Dogwood Park and Franklin Park, then along Patriot Boulevard. He still doesn't get why they changed the name from 88th Street to Patriot Boulevard—did they really think changing the name of a street would improve the neighborhood? He finally gets to Blake Street stop and exits the train, and since he didn't pay for the train, he can stop at the Package store and get some chips and a blunt. He knows somebody will have green—probably T.

Marcus gets to the studio and they smoke. It's Kenny's turn to pay the twenty dollars for the recording session, and Marcus is glad to see he has the money. Kenny's the one with the job—he stocks groceries at the Save-A-Lot, so he usually has something in his pocket. T and Kenny are talking about Latecia:

"She fucked me 'cause she like dark-skinned dudes. She fucked you 'cause she like light-skinned dudes and she fucked Danny 'cause she like white dudes," T says. Marcus gives them a "stop wasting time" look. His boys count on him to be the motivator.

"Let's get this shit started. What y'all wanna work on? Y'all got some new shit or you want to keep going with T's shit—that Grind shit," Marcus says.

"T, how that Grind shit go again?" asks Lenny.

"Hold on. Put the beat on."

"Naw, just spit it one time."

"Okay. It's like, yo, it's like,
Seems like I'm on the grind/
Ninety nine percent of the time/
One percent to eat/
Not one to sleep/
So drop me a line/
Let it flip my mind/
Back in to Go Mode/
No time for dro bro/
Until the cash flow/
Get back to equal."

"Did you hear that? No time for dro, bro, no time for dro, bro," Big Lenny repeats, smiling, once for each of his friends since they're lit and he doesn't smoke. Lenny's big and goofy and easy to get along with as long as you don't chill with him for too long.

Marcus, T, and Kenny take out their miniature notebooks and begin writing. Lenny follows suit. And then, after ten minutes, Marcus breaks the silence with his flow:

"I'm on the grind, with the folk tryin to catch me/
But I'm slick, dog, watch 'em mash right past me/
Thought I ran but I just ducked into the back seat/
They search my whip, but don't find shit 'cause I'm in a taxi/
That's just the facts, G/
I'm a mac, you see/
I been fuckin with the twelve, since I's about three/
And if they get me/
I make my decision quickly/

To do the time/
Or reach for my nine/
And give it my all/
Sprayin rounds til I fall/
Cause I'm a wild muthafucka that's ready to brawl"

He stops for a minute. Then says,

"And if that's how I go down/
Then that's how I go down/
But muthafuckas can't say I wasn't down to throw down."
"You snapped right there," Lil Kenny says as he gets up. He always stands when he raps:
"I'm on the grind like some coffee
Bitch get off me
You dress like me
you talk like me
But bitch you not me."
"Why would you rap about coffee, bruh?" Lenny says.
"It's a metaphor, dumbass. My mom drinks fresh coffee every day, bruh—you have to grind the beans before you make the coffee." They work on the Grind track for a while longer, and then Lenny changes the conversation to what they're going to wear when they get on 106 and Park.
"Nigga that's why you ain't spit nothing the whole time 'cause you sittin' here thinking about being famous when we ain't even made a CD yet!" Marcus says.
"You gotta believe in yourself," says Lenny. "I know though, I gotta get in Japanese mode. No bullshit." Marcus had seen this

video on the Japanese and it said they worked fifteen hours a day and even the kids did eight hours of homework a day. Ever since then, when they're really trying to get stuff done, they try to act like they're Japanese so they can at least do a couple hours straight of hard work. Right now, Lenny's getting into his Japanese posture, pretending that he's meditating. With his eyes closed, he begins quivering his head faster and faster, like his inner concentration is so focused that his head is going to explode. Everyone starts laughing, and then Lenny puts on a nerdy white boy voice, "but guys, can I have a turn now? Would that be all right? Please, guys? Can I please try a rap song?" He clears his throat so loud that the laughter stops. Then, changing into a more serious tone, he starts:

"I'm a ugly muthafucka, that's why I rap/
Why else you think these ladies ever let me tap?/
I'm telling you man/
This fame is some shit/
Turns my dick to a coke pole/
These bitches' clits to a nostrol/
They're fiends for me/
They cling to me/
It's like I'm God and they all practice Christianity."

"This fool..." Kenny shakes his head. "What the hell is a coke pole?"

"A pole made out of cocaine, nigga!"

"Shiiit—it's a good thing you don't drink or smoke, bruh, 'cause it's no telling what your crazy mind would come up with," Kenny says and starts laughing. Lenny doesn't drink because his mom's an alcoholic and he stopped smoking because he says it makes him paranoid.

"On everything, though, when I make it, I'ma be the rapper with the most kids," Lenny says, "'cause look, I'ma have the money, so why not have the chirrun? Have me like a hundred! 'Cause ain't nobody done that yet. Basically, you feel me, every good looking chick that's down, I'ma do it with—and I'ma be so rich that I could pay child support to all my baby mamas. It's gon be a army of lil Lennys!" He gazes up to the ceiling like he can picture it now.

"And they all gonna have STD's too. And you gon be the sergeant with AIDS, herpes, and gonorrhea!" Marcus says. "I ain't having babies till I'm twenty-five—I got too much to do, and I ain't being no dead beat neither. That's why I wrap my shit up every time. Shit. Talkin' bout it feels better raw—nigga, how it feel being a daddy without no money and the baby crying? Fuck that— pussy feel good enough with a rubber."

The next group starts coming in so they call it a day and walk outside.

"What y'all trying to do?" Kenny says.

"Get a bottle. Shit," Marcus says.

"How much you got on it?"

"You the one with the job, nigga."

"I got four," T says.

"What they say, you chill with three broke niggas, you gon be the fourth?" Kenny says. They walk to the package store, find somebody over twenty-one to buy them a fifth of Bacardi, and start the long walk home.

Chapter 8 – Nick

Nick gets out of the pickup and sees his mom arguing with Alex on the porch. The strange thing is that Alex is out of his room and is actually smiling. Nick is used to him being in his room, sleeping, staring at the ceiling, or listening to sports talk radio. Bipolar is no joke. "What's up dude," he says to Nick with a smirk on his face. It's the first time Nick's seen him smile in a long time.

"Don't 'What's up dude' him!" Mom says to Alex. She turns to Nick, "You know what your brother did last night? He went out spray-painting and ended up spending the night in jail because he got caught." Mom has a green smoothie in one hand and a cigarette in the other. "He thought your dad would come make everything okay like last time, but he didn't. They caught him spray-painting a billboard that said 'BIOTECH' across it and you know what he did? It was big blue letters with white in the back, and he goes over there with white spray paint and sprays out the letter "E" so the sign says 'BIOT CH.' I don't get 'biotch'? What is that, 'biotch'?"

"Yeah, dude. What is that biotch?" Nick says, smiling and shaking his head. He looks at his brother, who is trying to hide a little grin.

Their mom continues: "And when I asked why he risked so much to do something so stupid, he said, 'I thought it would be funny.' Yeah, real funny—about a thousand dollars' worth of funny—and now you have a record." She's trying to be mad, but isn't doing a very good job. She can't help but enjoy seeing her boys happy. And it's a sign that Alex is finally out of this episode of depression—and his dry skin, dark bowls under the eyes, and twitching nerves probably means he's starting a manic one. That's always how it is, once you're happy that he's finally out of bed, you're nervous about what the hell he's gonna do.

Alex returns from the kitchen with a leash, and Bingi, the Chihuahua, hears the jingle and comes running over, bouncing like a pogo stick in front of the door. The whole family is in the backyard already, so he starts saying hi to everyone and then his mom whispers for him to go with Alex, so he follows him outside. "Dude, how the fuck are you not cold right now?" Nick asks, looking down at Alex's corduroy shorts as they step down the icy porch.

"The air feels good," Alex says. It must be the medication that warms him. "Don't be a little puss. Have you been stealing any beers lately?" he asks.

"No, bro," Nick says, shaking his head. As they walk, Alex bumps against Nick's jacket every step—it's what he does when he zeroes in on the conversation, and it reminds Nick how much he loves his brother.

"I know you have, dude. You're fucking lying. I stole some yesterday—I love doing that crap. Remember when you stole that bottle of white wine and we drank it and then you threw the empty through the new Starbuck's window? Baaaaaaaaam—fuck Starbuck's. We should do that again tonight."

"Naw, bro. You just got arrested last night—you need to calm down."

Alex stops. He looks at Nick like Nick just took a dump on the sidewalk. "Are you telling me how to act, dude? I'm your older brother and I don't tell you how to act—why the *fuck* do you think you can tell me how to live my life?"

Bingi squats to pee on some grass as an old man opens the door. "If you don't clean up after your dog!" the man says, standing on his porch in his suspenders.

"Oh," Alex says, "Oh, oh, oh," moving like a robot, looking in a new direction with each "oh." He steps onto the man's lawn and squats down to where the dog peed. He does an exaggerated nod. "You want me to *wipe* the *urine* off your *grass*, sir?" he says. The old man shakes his head and shoos him away with his hand. Alex takes a few steps closer to him, now in the center of the lawn. "Let's make a deal. I'll wipe the grass," he says, looking back and forth between the wet area and the man, "if you wipe her pussy… Does that work? Is that a deal?"

No, *this* reminds Nick how much he loves his brother—and at the same time, how much he can't stand that crazy motherfucker.

Nick tugs at the back of Alex's tee shirt to pry him out of the situation and they continue walking around the block. It's always the same block with Alex. Same block, same direction, again and again.

Nick gets all the details on the bombing mission and Alex's arrest. He had climbed onto the Chinese restaurant and then up to the billboard and was halfway done painting when the cops came.

"So you didn't get to finish it?" Nick says as they lap their house and keep walking.

"I finished it. The police snuck up on me and were just watching me paint for a while. They were actually shining their flashlights at the billboard to help me paint. Then they started yelling and I told them I was almost done. I told them how to climb up, too. And they tried, but they were too fat, so they just waited for me to finish."

"Waiting for you to finish?" Nick searches for the right words. "Bro. Come on. They weren't waiting for you to finish and they weren't helping you paint. You *really* fucked up."

Alex steps back from Nick and stops walking. "If you do this one more time I'm going home. Did I tell you that you fucked up throwing that bottle through Starbucks?" He waits a second, looks down with his eyes squeezed and his neck strained to the left. "Exactly. Don't question my life, dude. I was in jail—I served time," Alex says.

"You were in a holding cell for one night, bro," Nick says. "All I'm saying is I worry about you. Mom worries about you," he adds.

"And that's the problem. You worry too much. You and mom worrying actually makes me worse. You realize that, right? You guys cause me to be the way I am. If you would stop worrying, I would get better," Alex says.

No response needed. As they round the corner, they see the old man again. He's sitting on the fucking stoop. Just sitting there, pretending that he's enjoying the cold-ass weather.

Bingi walks up to the spot where she peed, smells it, and then squats, looks back and forth from the man to Nick and Alex, and flexes out a three inch turd. This cannot be happening. She uproots a few blades of grass with her hind feet and then prances as far as the leash allows her.

Nick looks at Alex and sees that he doesn't have a bag… Fuck. The old man doesn't need to say anything. He's shaking his head like he's worried about the whole future generation. Nick pats all of his pockets, knowing damn well that he doesn't have a bag.

"This is a free service," Alex says. "We provide fertilizer for your grass at no charge."

"Hey!" Nick tries to snap Alex out of it.

"It's free for all senior citizens because when you get to be a geezer you don't know how to do anything but spy on people, yell at kids, and ruin people's lives when they just want to walk around the fucking block and clear their head. This tiny little piece of poop is the most important thing in your whole day—don't you see a problem with that?"

"Hey!" Nick says, getting inches from Alex's face and grabbing his shoulder. "Dude, that's a old man."

Alex snaps his head toward the ground. "Sorry sorry sorry sorry sorry," he trails off into a mumble. You can never tell what's going on in there. Inside his head. Because it's like he's on a ride that he can't control, and all you can do is try to jolt him out of it for a second or two.

"That's enough," says the old guy. "I'm done with you. You do nothing but walk around harassing me and my wife and making us pick up after your dog. I've had enough…"

"Sir!" Nick interrupts. "I'm sorry about my brother. He's…"

"I pick up after my dog and I respect my elders—that's how I was raised," Alex interjects. Then he opens his palm towards Nick like a golfer to his caddy. "Nick—cigarettes," he says, eyes still on the man.

"What? Let's get out of here."

"Give me your cigarettes," Alex repeats.

"What are you talking about? You're smoking now?" Nick says, but obeys his big brother and lifts the Dorals from his pocket and hands them over.

Alex holds the top of the box and slides the cellophane off the bottom. He carefully pushes the plastic inside out with his pointer and thumb, and proceeds to bend over, pinch the warm, soft little log into the plastic, and then reverses the edges so the miniature poop drops into the cup of the miniature bag. He holds it in the air, steam still rising, and tilts his raised fingers back while bowing his head for forgiveness.

They continue on their walk. Alex's pace is fast. His thick, long legs are speed walking ahead. Bingi's tiny legs struggle to keep up with the tug on her collar, and Alex is oblivious to both her and Nick. The tiny sack of shit falls from his left hand onto the sidewalk, and Nick considers saying something, but then reminds himself that he needs to choose his battles, so he checks for peeping neighbors and then pretends he doesn't see it.

They finish the second lap and Nick convinces Alex to come inside.

Chapter 9 – Quintavious

"Hold up," Quint says, leaning against the cinderblocks lining the stairwell. "I gotta catch my breath."

"Damn, nigga, you out of shape. It's only one more flight of stairs till we at the top," Marcus says as he passes his brother, taking three steps at a time.

"What happened to smoking in the park like a normal person?" Quint says. Why does Marcus always have to make shit difficult.

"Naw. I can't believe you never been to The Office. Me and Kenny been coming up here for years," Marcus says, looking down from the doorway of the roof like he's a motherfucking fitness trainer or some shit. Quint struggles to make it up the last ten steps, but the sunlight streaming down the stairwell lands on his face and motivates him. He can even hear birds.

"Why y'all call it The Office?" Quint says as he hoists his leg up the final step and then bends over, hands on his knees. The bright sun and sharp cold air feel good on his sweaty skin. He stares at the tiny rocks on the roof's surface.

"We was higher than a bitch up here one time, talking about what would it be like to come to a computer job every day, like they do in this building."

"Oh," Quint says, still hunched.

"Damn, nigga, you look like you're about to have a asthma attack—you need to shed some pounds, for real."

"Nigga you need to gain some pounds—I could practically see your bones poking out that shirt." Quint says. He looks at his little brother and can tell right away that he's gonna try some shit—the expression on Marcus's face—it's the eyebrows. It must be the eyebrows that gives him away, but before he can get his body to stand up straight, Marcus has established slap-boxing position and then lands a quick one across his cheek and takes an even quicker step backwards. "Try that one more time. Lord, I pray this little nigga tries that just one more time!" Quint says, smiling and slowly shaking his head as he steps towards his baby brother. Marcus returns the smile. And then, just as Quint is going to use that older brother advantage, Marcus comes charging towards him, wrapping his arms around Quint as fast as he can. He tries to lift but Quint kicks his left leg back, widening his stance and lowering his body weight. Marcus tries again to jolt his big brother up, feels him tilt, but then Quint reaches over Marcus, wrapping him up in an upside down grip, and then flips him head under heels and then whole body bammed, onto the roof.

The two brothers lie head by head, bodies straight out on either side like hands on a clock.

They look at the sky and breathe. And look. And breathe. And look. Minutes go by. Just staring.

"He ain't never coming back," Quint says. "He ain't never coming back. Because of something I did."

"Nigga shut up," Marcus says.

"I kilt Dad, bruh. If I didn't steal nothing, Dad still be here." Quint sucks his cheeks between his top and bottom teeth. His forehead is scrunched up.

"Cracker police killed Dad! You stole some candy from the gas station, man! Everybody do that. Who *don't* do that? Shit. They tased a ten year-old child for stealing candy! They took Dad from us…"

"I didn't need to steal that candy and I didn't need to run to the house and Dad didn't need to go at the police."

"Ain't nobody perfect, Quint. You made a regular mistake and they murdered Dad. They took Dad from us. They took his life from him. Don't twist that shit around. It's not time to feel bad. It's time to let them get a taste. I'm saying. I remember that cop. I know exactly who he is. I know his beat and everything. Bruh, I've thought about this again and again. Sometimes you gotta do things you don't feel like doing. Justice don't just happen by itself—you gotta stand up and make it happen—bodies with badges. Let they family get a taste. See how it feel."

"I miss Dad, man," Quint breathes hard and reaches his fingers to his face and pinches tears out of his eyes and onto the bridge of his nose and then onto his fingertips. "Remember how we used to do Wrestle Mania in the TV room? Dad used to be in the middle of the rug on his knees, talking about 'No one can de-thrown the KING!' and we used to double-team him, hanging on his shoulders. He be picking us up, both at the same time, and throwing us onto the couch." Q swallows.

"Hell yeah," says Marcus. "Dad's buff-ass—didn't nobody fuck with Dad, boy." He smiles.

"But you feel me, you doing something to that cop ain't gonna do nothing. It's over. All you end up doing is catching a case. You just doing the same thing I did and the same thing Dad did. Making a bad decision."

Marcus throws his head up. "It ain't the same thing! That's what they want you to think! They don't want niggas to fight back. They want you to be scared. I'm telling you." He sits up and starts throwing chips of rock at an aluminum air duct protruding from the rooftop. Quint stays on his back, not saying anything. "Did you bring that lighter though?"

"Yeah, I got it," Quint says.

Marcus pulls out a dime bag and a White Owl and starts breaking down the weed.

Chapter 10 – Nick

Nick walks up the steps to his apartment. Muffled voices hit his ears, and they aren't coming from Todd's place. He lifts his chin and stands perfectly still. Is that Alex? Is that motherfucking Alex?

The door is locked so he uses his key to unlock it. Sitting on the couch is a big woman with fake blond hair, hoop earrings the size of a grapefruit, and a shirt so tight that the fabric disappears and reappears with the rolls on her sides. Alex is point blank in front of her talking about how he really does love her, leaning into her face while his ass weighs down the coffee table. She looks at Nick like she wants assistance, with her thick coat of make-up stretching and cracking as her painted-on eyebrows elevate to her hairline. Alex raises his hand and redirects her face towards his.

"Don't pay attention to him," Alex says, his back still towards Nick. "It's only me and you. That's all that matters right now."

"What are you doing here?" Nick says. "And what the hell is *she* doing here?"

"This is Bambi. This is… Can you leave us alone! We're trying to work on things and we're trying to figure things out and we're trying to…" Alex squeezes his eyes and shakes his spread out left hand next to his head like he's trying to erase Nick from the room. "Can you just leave us alone I can't believe you're barging in on us right now."

"I need to go and you need to pay me my thirty dollars," the woman says, gathering her things. She's trying to be professional but those dark, Sharpie-looking eyebrows scrunch together so much that it looks like there's an invisible clothespin clamped on her forehead.

"That's all you talk about is money like you miss the whole fucking point of what we talk about and the connection that we have," Alex says. "Don't pay attention to him—he does not matter at all. Pay attention to what we talked about. Like the important stuff. Remember? Remember when you said you don't want to have kids and I said I don't want to have kids because we don't want to bring them into this world the way it is and knowing that they would have to go through the same things we went through. Don't just change the subject because my brother is here why do people do that right when a person comes in the room?" Alex takes a loud breath. "They change the way they act just because a person's here, when they don't even know that person and they don't give a fuck about him. Bambi you don't give a fuck about my brother and now you want to be a prissy 'pay me my money' type

59

of girl just because he's here? Really, baby? You're pulling this card right now."

"It's okay. Al. Al. Let her go. It's okay. Do you have the money you owe her?"

"The money *I* owe *her*? More like the other way around. But we turned that corner a long time ago. If she wants money, I give her money. But trust me, that's not what this situation is about."

Nick feels his pockets but knows he only has six dollars.

"Do you need money, baby?" Alex asks.

"Yeah. You owe me money," she says, her top lip raised. She's holding her big, knock-off Louis Vuitton purse with both hands in the center of her lap.

"Okay don't talk to me like I'm stupid. You don't talk to anybody else like that. And don't talk to my brother like he knows everything. He's my little brother. *Little* brother. You realize that, right?" Alex says. "How much money do you need?"

"Thirty."

"Okay." Alex sits up straight and reaches in his pockets. "Here's forty… Now was that really that hard? If you need money, then I give it to you. If I need money, you give it to me. That's how a relationship works."

"Bye," she says, and stands. Alex reaches for her arm to restrain her.

"Al!" Nick snaps. Alex's arm recoils instinctually and he looks at his brother for the first time—eyes like he just woke up. "Let her go."

Bambi passes Nick in the doorway. "You need to help him," she says.

"Oh, really?" Nick says, and closes the door.

Alex gets up and paces. "Fuck. You," he says.

"Fuck me? Bro. You bring a prostitute back to my house and then you're mad at me?"

"Can you shut, the hell, up, about her being a prostitute? Can you stop judging everyone you see?"

"Whatever, dude, you just fucked a ho in my bed, broke into my house…"

"Broke into your house? I'm your brother. Since when can a brother not go to his brother's house? Now I'm a criminal because I found your key under the fake rock that me and Mom bought you for Christmas? You think you understand everything about everybody. You think everybody's just like you. Everyone wants to just go out, start a family. Have babies. I don't want to have babies. Bambi doesn't want to have babies. That's why we connect like we do. Do you ever think about us?"

Alex shakes his head from side to side, blinking quickly. "I'm not gonna bring a child into this world and have them go through what I've gone through. I swear I would never wish this on anyone." And now Nick knows he's talking about his mental illness. "Never. I pray to God it never hits you because this thing is like nothing you've experienced, dude." His eyes open wide, looking at nothing at all, and his head slows to a stop. "I'm serious."

Nick reaches over and rubs his brother's back. "I know, man. It's fucked up," he says. And he doesn't know what else to say—it's been six years of this roller-coaster since the condition took over Alex's mind his sophomore year in college. "But here's what you gotta do—stay on your meds and do what they say you need to do. You're gonna get through it, all right?" It's all he can say. It's all he can hope for—even though he doesn't know if it's true or not. He rubs his brother's back and watches his face shudder to the left and his eyes shut—sees him grimace and his eyes twitch.

After five minutes, Alex turns to Nick. "Let's go to the store and get some forties. Do you have some money?"

"I'm dead broke," Nick says. He considers putting Alex on the bus back to Mom's but doesn't want to take the risk. "Let's play UNO. You ready to get your ass whipped?"

"You wish," Alex says, and picks up the pack of cards from on top of the TV. "If I win, we go get forties and Bambi can come back here."

"Just shuffle the fucking deck."

Chapter 11 – Marcus

Marcus opens his eyes. What happened? What is he doing? Where is he going?

He looks at his legs as if he weren't controlling them. Because he's walking! The last thing he remembered, he was sleeping, and dreaming. Now he's walking. Outside. He looks at his body and realizes that he is sleepwalking. *Was* sleepwalking—now is really walking. And somehow he had put sweatpants and Timberlands on! Not exactly enough to keep him warm, but at least he's clothed.

It's the middle of the night sometime, and nobody's out. Marcus gets his bearings and turns to walk the two blocks back to the house, but then he checks his pockets, and fuck, there are no keys.

He stands still—his mind rhythmically stirring in circles. He should go back and throw rocks at Quint's window to wake him up and let him in. Or no… Actually, why not wander the neighborhood, see where his legs will steer him. The deserted neighborhood feels like a dream but the sharp air gives him clarity—a combination that he's never felt. Could it be a dream? Maybe it's one of those dreams you can control—Marcus smiles as he walks. He loves those. He decides to test it out. He always tests it out the same way. First, he tries creating a naked woman behind a parked car and then walks around the rear bumper to see if it worked—no luck. Time to try step two—try to fly. He wills his body into the air to take flight, but as he suspected, no luck. Better not to think about it. Better to ride this one out. He observes his legs carrying him through the silver landscape—down Juniper Street, past the Citgo. His feet lead him to the right, through the cut, then left on 82nd. He knows where he's going. He slows down as he approaches the lawn. Walks up to the edge of the sidewalk. He looks back to the right and sees the chain link gate. There are new people living in the house now. There have *been* new people living in the house. They changed the path going to the gate—they put woodchips and slabs of stone to walk on—but it's still the same gate. Marcus floats towards it, but suddenly can't move. It's like he's controlling himself in a videogame and he's gone to the edge of the map. His controller says forward but his figure doesn't budge. And he knows where he is. Exactly where he is. He's standing in the cop's footprints. Exactly where the cop was when he pulled his taser out and shot Quintavious. Marcus is frozen—the only thing he can move are his eyeballs. And then his breath. He feels his breath pressing against the back of his front teeth. And then his legs crackle and movement slowly resumes.

He can't help but continue towards the gate. A motion sensor surveillance light turns on, but it does not deter him. He averts his eyes from the motherfucking floodlight interrogation light and focuses down on the woodchips—they're sharp with contrast, silver red and pitch black shadows speckle the ground.

He looks away. Looks at the lawn. Stares at the spot. That one spot. If that one spot didn't exist, none of this would have happened. That one spot. The cause and effect of all the evil and injustice in the world. He stands and watches the movie again. Straight faced. It happens again—all of it, in random flashes—Dad lying there, bloody and still, Dad charging the cop, Dad having his hands raised in surrender, Dad getting plugged full of bullets by the cowards behind the car doors, them getting shuttled away from the scene, Mama with the scream that pierced the air like the devil was an inch from her face, the scream that ended the world, that got neighbors out of houses faster than the gun shots, shrieking and running out and falling on Dad, trying to lift his heavy chest, buckling in his blood. He sees it all right now—like he's seen it a million times.

And now all senses are there. Marcus is no longer controlling himself, but is fully himself. His strength, all of his strength, drains into the soil underneath the grass, and he collapses onto his knees. The backs of his hands land on the ground like a final act of surrender. He lets his eyes go—tears sliding down over his mouth. And he feels something. Something. Like Dad is there. Like Dad's spirit is coming back to be with him.

And he hears the latch and whine of the front door of the house opening. It doesn't startle him. It's like he knew it was coming. Whatever. Let them do what they gotta do. They already stole the house, what more do they want? He waits and then turns his head and sees who it is. It's a dark-skinned old man, at least eighty, in a black bathrobe, standing in front of the door. Fuck him. "Yeah?" Marcus says. "You just gonna stand there?"

"You need help with something?" the man says, calm and smooth.

"Can I help *you* with something?"

"Well, you are on *my* lawn. You did wake up *my* wife—I'm sitting here wondering what you're doing."

"So now this is your lawn?" Marcus says straight to the man, his body shaking in the cold. "You own it? You own the blades of grass? The roots reaching down? And you know what them roots are sucking? Not water—they sucking straight blood. Do you realize that? Straight up blood. From my dad. That's what it is. But you own it. And that blood is *why* you own it. It's down here." Marcus reaches down and digs his fingernails through the grass and soil and clenches a fistful. "From when it was *my* grass. And you telling me it's *your* grass and I can't walk here." He shivers. The old man shuts the door behind him and puts his hands in the pockets of his robe. What a sorry motherfucker. "So when you get murdered by the police, right here, guess what's gonna happen to your wife? Your kids? Huh?" Marcus continues. "Shit won't never be the same." He spits into the lawn.

"What's your father's name?" the old man asks.

"My dad name *was* Bobby Jones."

"Bobby Jones, huh? Bobby Jones," the man says, and Marcus realizes that he hadn't heard or said his dad's name in a while. "I think he was a good man. And I think he had a good son."

Marcus's neck swells up. "That's my dad," he whispers, not to the old man, but into the air, staring at the patch of lawn. "He believed in me. That I had potential." Marcus closes his eyes. "That was you, Dad. I remember when you asked me, do I think I have potential. I said yeah. And you said if it's ever a one percent chance that you think you got potential to do something, to make a change, to do something big, like something positive, that then… then you got responsibility. Potential turns into responsibility." *Potential turns into responsibility…* The words loop and bounce through his mind and his mouth. "To yourself and to God. To put in work. The burden and the blessing of potential." He doesn't blink, but stares at the air between him and the grass. "You had faith in me." And he feels his dad with him, through him. And it's all love. And it feels so good. "I'll do right by you, though. Watch. I know what you want me to do. And if I do it, then that's you living on, through me and Quint. Responsibil…"

Marcus closes his eyes and feels complete. Like he's eaten a meal after days of starvation. The old man is all right. He should show him some respect and say thank you to him. Show his appreciation. But where'd he go? The steps in front of the door are empty—the door shut.

His grip loosens on the clump of earth and chunks fall down his leg as he leaves his old house to return home. He's a warrior coated by the orange of the sunrise.

Chapter 12 — Quintavious

Quint comes up to the park with his two pits, Drama and Dora, and sees that T and Psycho are drinking a bottle at the playground. Psycho and T are both Marcus's age, but Quint has always chilled with them just the same.

"Can I drink with you, my niggas?" Q says. T hands him the bottle of gin and he takes a swig.

"Where's your Mark-ass brother? I stopped by the house and wasn't nobody there," T says, repeating the same joke he's been saying forever. But that's how T is. He finds something he likes and sticks with it. He's a man of routine. Like the way he sells drugs. He sells to put money in his pocket, but that's it. It's not like he's trying to move up in the game. And he's the same way with women—being with them but never having a relationship. It doesn't hurt that he's a pretty boy. He's got the smile and the smooth, dark skin—they just love that.

"I don't know where he at—I ain't his P.O. bruh," Q says as he pulls a Newport 100 from his ear and lights it.

"Short," T says.

"Deuce," Psycho calls. He's playing with Drama—holding onto a chew rope, wrenching it back and forth as she grips with her jaw. Drama's stronger than Dora—when Quint plays with her, he'll hold the stretch of rope in two hands, elbows towards the ground, and Drama will jump and clamp onto the middle. He'll hold her there and then do curls, like he's lifting weights, while she growls through the sides of her mouth. Psycho is trying to replicate the trick, but is unsuccessful. He gets frustrated and starts whipping the knotted end of rope into the side of Drama's head. Q keeps his eye on him. Psycho *will* be psycho.

T takes the half cigarette from Q, drags it a few times, and then passes it to Psycho for the last couple. They keep drinking the bottle and Psycho keeps fucking with the dogs. He's shaking the rope and running up onto the play structure with both dogs chasing after him, and then down the bright orange slide—the dogs half running and half sliding after him. "God damn, this is a workout, bruh!" he yells.

"That ain't a workout, nigga, you just out of shape," T says. "Overweight. Can't walk straight," then starts mumbling rhymes under his breath.

"I need a drink—all this exercise—for real!" Psycho says, panting and reaching out for the bottle. He feels the weight of the bottle and then lifts it from the paper bag to see how much is left. "God damn, y'all are wrong for that. Fuck that—see if I ever play with your punk-ass dogs again." He shakes his head, takes the last inch and a half of gin to the neck and then throws the empty into the bushes, looks down with a scrunched-up face and shakes his head back and forth in pain.

"Damn, bruh, you didn't have to kill it," Quint says.

Psycho is still shaking his head. "Suckmydick," he says, grimacing.

"Ay, there goes fine-ass Shawnese. Shawnese!" Q yells as she walks down the sidewalk next to the park. "What's up girl?"

"What's up Q?"

"Just enjoying the day—thinking about you. Come chill for a minute."

"Stop playing," she giggles. "I can't. I gotta go to work. I holler at you."

"She's a fucking quarter piece right there," Psycho says. "You saw how she was looking at me?"

"I'd fuck the shit out of her," T says.

"I know I would. I'd *love* to fuck her," Q says.

"If I had to eat pussy, my nigga, I'd eat her pussy," Psycho says.

"You'd eat that pussy if you didn't have to."

"I swear to God, bruh, I never ate pussy," Psycho says. "But I'll tell you one thing. Sometimes I be feeling like doing that shit, dog. When they be looking so sweet and you be kissing on 'em, I just wanna lickemup!"

"Hell naw," T says. "I know Q be eating that pussy. Huh Q?"

Q looks to either side of him like he's scoping for bystanders, licks his lips and gets this grown man, I'm-the-wise-one look on his face. "Let me tell y'all lil young bloods something. When you get to be my age, and you get you a real girl." He starts nodding his head. "You gonna take a few licks here and there. I'm not talking about doing that thing all the time, or, you know, for like forty-five minutes straight—hell naw, a nigga tongue get tired. But I'm telling you, go down there every once in a while, when it just feel right, and you give a couple licks and then feel her start to move around and start breathing hard. Boy, I'm telling you. She starts feeling on your head and shit, then tells you to hurry up and stick it in. Nigga that's some good sex."

"Naw, you won't catch me doing that shit," T says, smiling.

"With all the nasty hoes you be fucking, I wouldn't either. T got the dirtiest dick in the city."

"That's my dick, not my tongue though," T says. Suddenly the dogs start growling and they all look over and see Old Roy. Old Roy's a nervous crackhead who's looking to buy a rock off T.

"Get your dogs, Quint. Can you please get your dogs," Old Roy says with big eyes and a scared look on his face.

"Man my dogs ain't gonna do shit. If you just cool out maybe they'll stop barking, your old twitchin' ass." Q snaps his fingers and calls his dogs' names quietly and they come over to him, tails wagging. His dad always taught him that you should never have to raise your voice at a dog. He remembers that. His dad could give the dogs a look and a nod and they would go lay down.

T takes Old Roy's money and goes over to the bench where his stash is hidden in a crumpled paper bag and gets him a five-bag. Old Roy tries to say it's short but T tells him to get the hell on and he does.

"I'm trying to drink some more—what's up with the college kegs?" Psycho says.

"Let's do it," T says.

"T-t-t-totally dude," Psycho says, and they start walking up Patriot Blvd toward the neighborhood where all the university students live. T decides to get some food and stops at China Life to get some chicken fried rice. He eats half and then lets Psycho and Quint finish it.

They walk by Quint's house to drop off the dogs and Marcus is outside eating some noodles. Quint puts the dogs inside and then comes out to the group. A small white car rolls up to them with a chubby white boy in it. They can already tell he's a university student looking for some drugs. His eyes spell buster as he nods what's up. "Hey, you guys got any blow?" he asks.

Marcus walks up to the window. "How much you looking for?"

"Um, just like a twenty for now," he says.

"Yeah I gotchu," Marcus says, holding out his hand for the money.

"Can I see it first?"

"This the fire, man, let me hold the dub 'cause I gotta go right in that door and get it from my man. I be back in thirty seconds—my homeboy will stay right here with you." The boy hesitates but gives him the twenty dollar bill. Marcus steps back from the window of the car, puts the money in his jacket pocket, takes a bite of noodles, and stares at the boy. His face turns from friendly to serious to disgusted. "Go home," he says and nods his head in the direction the boy needs to drive. Psycho is laughing and hanging his body weight on T's shoulders.

"Why does it have to be like that? Man, that's fucking lame," the boy says and drives off.

Quint looks at Marcus. There's something not right about the way he's been lately. And he knows what it is. Marcus is going to try to get the cop. He's going to do it soon. There's no way of talking him out of it—he doesn't respond to anything these days. There's a certain point where you gotta let a man live his life and live with the consequences of his actions. But he *is* still family. "Is you really that stupid?" Q says, staring at his brother, who avoids eye contact. "You gonna rob somebody right in front of the house?"

"It's just too easy," Marcus says, smiling at Psycho and taking another bite of noodles. "They just make it so easy."

Marcus decides to stay back, but Psycho, Quint, and T walk around the south side of Frazier Lake going east toward the parties. The west side of the lake is considered the bad side and you might see some people jogging around there on a really nice day, but for the most part, only people from the west side hang out on the west side. The east side of the lake, which is by all the bourgie stores and restaurants, is where you see all kinds of people having picnics and cookouts and bringing their kids to play on the playground. You'll never see anyone swimming in the lake though; it's not that kind of lake. Frazier lake was man-made about thirty years ago to try to improve the city—the only people that ever go in the lake are dead ones that get tossed in there.

Quint finds a rock and launches it into the air. It lands and disappears into the snowy cover on the lake. As he talks shit to Psycho, a bop comes up to T, buys a four-dollar bag and asks if any of them want some head for five. They all say they're straight and keep moving. Psycho and Quint continue throwing rocks through the frozen surface of the lake—it helps to do something to stay warm.

Even though T is only nineteen, he grew up fast and he tries to always stay on his game—so you won't catch him doing playful shit that often. When they branch off from the lake, T gets a call for some green so they go back down to 88th and he drops off a quarter for thirty to one of his homeboys, who will either flip it for thirty-five or break it up and sell it.

T buys a forty of Icehouse, Psycho buys some Newports, and they head down the main party blocks. It's dead and it's almost eleven on a Friday night. This isn't right—all they've seen so far is a little ten-person get-together, and it's getting cold so they're thinking about going up to the bars and seeing what's going on around there.

"Ay, let's go to Ashland right quick," Psycho says. So they walk down 76th to Ashland Street and within a few blocks they see people in bathrobes and bright towels running into the front door of a house. "I knew it! It's that house with the green light—they got some crazy parties, boy! And let me hold a dime—flip it for dub." It was easy to sell nickels for dimes at college parties.

"Nigga just send them my way. I'll deal with it."

"All right." They walk into the house. Inside they have the heat turned up all the way, some oldies playing on the stereo, and over half the party is dressed in swimsuits, fake flower lays, bath-robes, flip flops, and towels. "This a Baywatch party?" T says.

"I guess," Quint says. "And I'm not mad, neither." They make their way downstairs to the basement where the keg is. They're charging two dollars for a cup and Q and Psycho convince T to buy them all cups since he just made some sales. Sometimes they won't pay and just find cups around the party, but this party seems good and they don't want the college kids to find a reason to kick them out. They post up near the keg and start drinking their beer and talking. Meanwhile, people are playing beer-pong at a table in the basement.

"All right it's on, look at all these college girls. I wish I went to college, 'cause goddamn!" Psycho says.

T is so hot that he strips down to his wife beater and black jeans. He must think that fits into the beach thing better than his hooded jacket anyway. One girl passes him and looks up at him with a polite smile. "What's up with you, mama?" he says. She's wearing a blue bikini with white flip-flops and white sunglasses resting on her head.

"Nothin, what's up with you?" she says in a nervous voice, trying not to be racist.

"Just chillin. You play that game over there?"

"Sometimes, but I suck. I think I've made it in the cup like once in my whole life. Are you guys gonna play?"

"Maybe later on."

"Cool. Well if I decide to play I might need to recruit you to be my teammate, kay?"

"All right," he says, smiling.

Quint is over by the keg talking with a few guys in Hawaiian shirts. "Yeah, we grew up around here," Q says to a guy in a Hawaiian shirt who is holding a boogie board. "But I've been coming to the college parties for years—y'all know how to throw some parties. And plus, I only been to a couple that the police broke up and I don't think I ever seen a fight around here. That's what I like about these parties, everybody just have a good time."

"I know. I was upstairs and this girl was like, 'Okay, the thugs are here. Make sure you put your CDs away and keep an eye on your rooms.' I was like oh my God—that's so judgmental. Like, what, if you're not getting your higher education then you're not allowed to hang out with us? I mean, come on—isn't Jim Crow over?" he laughs. Q is surprised that some bitch upstairs said that, but his crew *has* been known to come up on CDs and other valuables at these kinds of parties.

"Yeah I get along with everybody—white, black, Mexican, whatever, you feel me? Just kick back and have a good time, it don't gotta be all that drama."

"I know, dude. It's ridiculous," he says, drinking his beer with excitement and nearly swinging his boogie board into someone. "I feel the same way. Like, why does everybody think there has to be drama like all the time? I mean, if you're always thinking about there being drama, then there's gonna be drama, you know? It's like, why can't people just take a chill pill and like chill out, you know what I mean?"

Q is thinking that he doesn't really care what this dude means when someone catches his eye. He squints his eyes a little more and makes sure it is who he thinks it is. Yep, it's the girl who he ran into last week who was throwing up—Ramona—the one who looks like the girl from Friends. Now she doesn't look so much like her, he must have been twisted, but there's still something about her. She's got a turquoise wrap thing around her booty and like a reddish orange swimsuit top. She doesn't even look his way as she walks across the basement to one of her girlfriends. Quint goes over to T.

"Ay, blood, that's that girl I was telling you about—that one I saw after I had left y'all on Saturday."

"What that one right there with the umbrella in her cup, in the blue?"

"Yeah." She's holding some Mickey Mouse kid's cup with a little umbrella poking out of the top.

"She do got a little boonky on her, I'll give you that." T was the type of dude that only looked at the ass on a girl. And it's funny, too, cause he's a good-looking dude and some top-notch females try to talk to him.

Q drinks another beer and then says, "watch how a player do it," pats T on the cheek and walks across the basement to Ramona.

Luckily she's not talking to anyone. "So I thought you said you was never gonna drink again," Q says with a smile. Ramona looks up at him like she knows she's seen him somewhere but can't remember where. He reminds her of the time, location, as well as the vomit.

"Oh my God," she blushes, "I remember that, sort of. You were so sweet to help me out." She turns to her friend. "I was totally wasted last Saturday and was seriously like on all fours throwing up in the snow and he came up and made sure I was okay and everything. Right?" She looks back up at Quint, wanting him to confirm the facts. "I didn't tell you you looked like R. Kelly did I?" she asks with a guilty look on her face.

"Yeah you actually said Robert Kelly."

"Oh my God I'm so sorry I said that—that's really bad."

"It's all good. I was just trying to make sure you made it inside all right.

"Thank you, I really appreciate that—do you go to the University?" Quint's never been asked that before. And even though it's obvious that he probably doesn't go there, he appreciates someone asking him.

"Naw, I just grew up in this neighborhood."

Quint and Ramona talk for a little while longer but Q doesn't want to act sprung, so he goes over to see how T is doing. Meanwhile, Psycho is sitting on an old trunk in the basement, drunk enough so he doesn't care that he has no one to talk to. Quint watches as the boogie board dude comes up to Psycho. "What's up man?" the beach boy says. "What's your name?"

"Psycho."

The kid starts laughing. "Yeah dude, I'm Wiiiild Mannn," he says with a shit-eating grin and eyes that match. Psycho just stares at him like *if you say one more word I'm gonna take your head off and shit down your neck.* The boy realizes he isn't playing and changes his tone. "So do you go to school, or work, or?" he says.

"Work."

"Very cool. What kind of work?"

Psycho takes a few seconds to think. "I'm a professional mover."

"Oh, so you help people move?"

"Yeah, I move things for people for a cut of the profit."

"Interesting! Do you have a crew of guys that work with you or for you?"

"Umm, a little bit. But it's mostly just me."

"Really? How do you handle big pieces of furniture?"

"I don't really handle it like that. But I handle it. And I don't really do furniture. But I *can* move furniture. Shit, I move whatever

the fuck you got: furniture, cars, jewelry, god damn, electronics…
shit… hard, soft, green—what the fuck you need me to move?"

"Oh, yeah, cool. Okay. Nothing—I was just, asking," the boy
says. "That's the bomb." He leaves. Psycho sits there, unaware that
Q heard the conversation. Quint is just happy Psycho used his
words instead of his hands.

It's so fucking hot down in the basement but Q can't take his
shirt off—can't strip down to his undershirt. He'd have to hit the
gym for a while before he felt okay about doing that. Instead, he
takes the bottom of his tank top from under the sweatshirt and uses
it like a napkin to wipe the sweat from his face. He suddenly hears
Ramona's voice behind him. She's talking to a guy about the protest she's going to in D.C. The guy tells her that she should appreciate what the government does for her. "Like, if you don't like the
way the U.S. is doing things, no offense, but why don't you just
leave and live somewhere else?" he asks.

"Well, sometimes I do think about living somewhere else," she
says. "But that won't help the situation. We need to dismantle the
oppressive systems in this country—if everybody who wants
change just leaves, it will just do the opposite. Does that make
sense?" *Get 'im, girl!* Q thinks. The two keep talking but the boy's
not really hearing her and it starts to get on Ramona's nerves so she
tells him she needs to pee.

The party is in high gear. There's a skinny boy and a big girl
wrestling by the beer-pong table, which, by this point, has no more
beer-pong balls on it. It's now just a table scattered with keg cups
filled with an inch of old beer and cigarette butts. Ramona comes
back from the bathroom. "Hey Quintavious!" she says, getting joy
out of each syllable. "I want to show my friend who my rescuer

was. Seriously, Rosie, I probably would've died if old Robert Kelly over here, just kidding, wouldn't have come to my rescue."

"Hey, let me tell you," Quint says to Ramona's friend. "Your homegirl wasn't making no kind of sense. I swear, when I walked up to her I thought *I* was drunk. But after all the mess she was talking about? Shit, she made me feel sober as hell."

"He really did rescue me. I would've been a little snowman by the morning. But Quintavious came to my rescue. I swear, Quintavious, if you ever need someone to like, hold your hair back so you can throw up or anything? Let me know. No, I'm serious—that was so sweet what you did, 'cause I do remember you just standing there, in the middle of the cold night, waiting for me to hurry up." Ramona walks across the room and picks up a dusty purple crayon that is laying on the cement basement floor. She then grabs the cardboard from an empty six-pack of Mike's Hard Lemonade, rips off a big piece and writes her name and phone number for Quint.

"Quintavious, I mean it. When you feel like you just can't make it back inside, you've had too much… give me a call. I don't do cell phones but call my landline and I will be there."

"Okay." Quint tries to think of a little joke to say, but all he can come up with is comparing it to a get-out-of-jail-free card that he can cash in but he thinks she might take it the wrong way if he starts talking about her bailing him out of jail. "That'll work." He smiles.

Chapter 13 – Nick

"OH-KAY! We got a shit-talking white boy. He only been here a week and he already talking shit!" says Charles, Marcus's stepdad. He smiles and sucks air through his tongue and his top two teeth, which are crooked to the point of forming a tented V shape—it's a habit that Nick noticed the first time they met. Charles carries a four by eight foot sheet of Coroplast and moves it onto the work table to take measurements.

Nick fiddles with a new work order, trying to understand the directions for the sign. His job at RapidSigns is cool so far. They hired him in Production, so all he does is bullshit with Charles and Julio, make signs, and listen to music. He talks with zero customers per day.

"I'm serious," Charles says. "I rather be with a woman that's been with fifty men than a woman that's been with none. 'Cause guess what? An experienced woman is gon' be a freak nine times out of ten. She gon' know how to drop that thang 'cause she likes sex more than you do!"

"Naw, fool, a virgin chick," Julio says. "'Cause she ain't never had it. She's gonna want it so bad." He pauses. "Her pussy's gonna be so wet. So tight. And she ain't never been in that world. It's like you're opening a door into a whole new world."

"Shiiiit," Charles says as he lines up his straight edge and makes a cut with his blade.

"No, bro," Nick says, looking up from his work. "She won't know what to do or how to move. Trust me. I was with a virgin one time. She was into it, but she just didn't move with the motion or anything. She just laid back."

"She probably didn't want it," Julio says.

"She wanted it, bro," Nick says. "I make sure of that. I ask straight up, Do you want to have sex? You can't play around with that."

"You gotta take it slow, bro," Julio says like he's picturing it now. "You can't be rushing into that—you gotta wait and wait, bro. For real. Wait till she pulling *your* pants off. I'm serious, she'll be thinking you're the man after that."

"Maybe—I still prefer a freak. An experienced woman that can teach me the ropes. I'm a truth seeker."

"That's what you want. But you know what you gonna get, right?" Julio pauses, "Herpes."

"My doctor said if you look down there and there aren't any bumps, then you're okay," Nick says.

"Your doctor's on crack."

"Ay Nick, I'm telling you," Charles says. "You need to start weeding right to left. If Gary comes in and sees you doing that, your ass is going to be looking for another job. You heard me?"

Nick looks at his vinyl lettering and then changes directions. Weeding is what you do ninety percent of the time in Production—it's when you separate the vinyl lettering from the stenciled background. And Nick likes it—he's ADHD and it keeps him busy. He likes taking his blade and sticking the tip into the thin plastic, peeling away the background and having the crisp, backwards letters remain. Weeding reminds him of eating fruit roll-ups when he was a kid—the way he used to peel it off the thin film it came on.

He finishes weeding a "For Sale" real estate sign and begins transferring it onto the Coroplast when Gary walks in—a new hire trails behind him. As always, when Gary comes back, everybody stops the chatter, straightens their backs, and begins working more quickly. "I'm gonna give him a shot, Charles. If he screws up, he's out," Gary says as he introduces Marcus as the new guy. Charles's mouth spreads into a smile and his eyes sink warmly to the side as he recognizes his stepson joining the team. Marcus's face beams and his chest puffs in response.

"I got five other guys I could hire right now," Gary says. "So I want you to train him. And Nick." He looks at Nick. "You're still on that same fucking job? Jesus Christ, hurry the hell up—I'm not paying you to sit back here and play grab-ass with Julio." Julio shakes his head. Gary's alcoholic red face turns back to Charles. "How's the job coming? I need the whole order done before close tonight. And make sure that banner gets reprinted too. You gotta keep your eye on it. That printer cost me twenty K and the ink isn't cheap either. It prints 800 square feet an hour so you gotta watch it. If I see any of the new guys near it, they're fired."

"We got it," says Charles.

"Get Marcus started on weeding," Gary says, and then leaves.

Nick watches as Marcus and Charles lock eyes like they were separated twins being reunited. "Well all right. Look at this!" Charles says. "Finally decides to take 'ol Charles's advice. Steppin' up! Done moochin' off me and your mom. I like that!" He puts his hands on Marcus's shoulders and gives him a little shake. "And you know what that means, right?"

"What that mean?" Marcus says, still smiling—not wanting to show how proud he is that he got a job.

"That means I could finally go on unemployment again," Charles says and starts laughing.

"Shit—you know Mama won't play that. She gonna have you up and out the house before she leave for work—you know that. And if you try to do that shit you be doing…" Marcus turns so everyone can hear him—acting like he's been working there for a month already. "My mom would throw this nigga out the house to get a job, right? And this nigga would act like he was walking to the train, but as soon as her car left, he bring his ass right back to the house. Hell naw, you try that shit again and I'm snitchin'—watch."

"Get over here and let me show you how to weed."

"I know about weed."

"You better stop fucking around or your ass gonna get fired the same day you got hired. You think I'm playing," Charles says, and follows with a fatherly look that gets Marcus to come over and pay attention to his instructions.

Suddenly Nick sees all three heads turn toward the entrance, so he follows suit and cocks his head back. It's Luana, the front desk girl—her loud heels coupled with her perfect posture and tight ponytail command respect. When she speaks, she ignores everyone but Charles. "Did you guys finish the real estate job? Because they just called and need forty more yard signs by tonight."

"That's too much, Luana, you're killing me, you know I can't do that—I got two new guys back here that I'm still training. We can't do all that."

"I'll take care of it for you," Marcus says to her, his jacket still on. Luana looks and decides not to acknowledge him.

"Gary says we have to, okay? He said use the perfect press and it needs to be done by tonight—I don't have time to argue about it—I've had a frustrating day all day."

"Probably sexual frustration," Julio says.

Luana looks down at Julio with a shaming gaze. "Julio—masturbation doesn't count as sex, so you need to think about your own sexual frustration." Nick stares as she exits the production room.

"You know we love you, Luana!" Julio yells to her back.

"I don't think Luana's ever experienced a skinny white guy," Nick says to the guys.

"You love the sistas, don't you?" Charles says, smiling. Luana is half black and Filipina—she has light, greenish brownish eyes and black, black hair.

"He's a wigger," Julio says as he sets a completed sign in the pile.

Nick thinks seriously about making up a story of being with a black girl, but he wants to make a bigger point—something that's been bothering him—so he starts it off by telling the truth. "I've never even been with one," Nick says.

"You a black pussy virgin?" Julio says. "I'm a white pussy virgin."

"I'm a Asian pussy virgin," Charles says.

Nick feels a little better now that he has company, but he still wants to get his point across. "Whatever. It's always a Black guy with a white girl. You never see a Black girl with a white dude," he says, weeding the vinyl letters the wrong way.

"Julio—get this man a tissue. It must be haaaard being white," Charles says.

"You saying they just sposed to give you some pussy 'cause you a white boy?" Julio says.

"No!" Nick thinks. That's not what he's saying, is it? That sounds racist the way Julio put it. But he didn't mean it like that. He meant it like he just wishes they were more open to the option of being with a white guy. "You don't think there's a difference between the way white girls go with Black guys and the way Black girls go with white guys?"

Charles sucks a whistle through his teeth. "Why can't they do what they want? If they want to experiment, let them experiment."

"Exactly, bro," Nick says. "That's exactly what I'm saying. But why doesn't it go both ways—I mean Black chicks being with white guys."

Marcus leans back into the conversation. "Only them self-hatin' sistas go for the white boys."

"So you're telling me that you've never been with a white girl?" Nick asks.

"I have," Charles answers.

"I never have. But I might," Marcus says.

"You guys don't let your ladies do what they want, but you get to do what you want. That's not right, man—it's a two way highway."

"Double standard," Marcus corrects him. Nick is surprised that Marcus knows double standard, and then feels racist for thinking he wouldn't.

"I like the way Nick said it—two way highway," Charles says. He feels a little better.

"Any way you look at it, it's not right," he tries to clarify. "You try to control them, but don't let them control you."

"Whoa, whoa, whoa! Be easy, little guy. I could tell you never been with a black girl, 'cause if you did, you'd know that these black women do what they want. You can't control them!" Charles says. "Try to tell them what to do, and watch what happens. They gonna make they own decision—I'm telling you. And that's fine— I ain't got a problem with that. I don't judge nobody."

"They could do what they want, but they a sellout if they go off with a white boy," Marcus says. "If they just fuck a white boy, it's okay. That's the way niggas should be, too—don't go marrying no white girl."

"I think love can cross all boundaries," Nick says as he squats down so that his eyes are at table level. He blows the surface of his work area, clearing tiny strips of vinyl.

"Oh my God, bruh, did your mom feed you tofu growing up, with your hippie-ass?" Marcus says.

"No bro. Strictly tempeh," Nick says. There's no response. "Damn, it's my lunch break."

"I ain't took my lunch either," Marcus says.

Charles tells him to sit his ass down—that he just got hired ten minutes ago. As Nick cleans the rest of his work station and heads out, Trick Daddy's "I'm a Thug" comes on the radio. Nick starts rapping along. "Could it be my baggy jeans, or my gold teeth, that make me different from y'all? Ain't trippin', dog, but listen, dog, I'm raised a little different, y'all. I'm just doing my thang."

Marcus looks at Charles, who's smiling, and then back at Nick. "Damn, you a black dick-rider, huh Nick?"

Bobbing to the beat, Nick turns around. "Black pussy-rider," he says, kissing the air in Marcus's direction, and then smiles. They shake their heads, laugh, and tell Nick to get the fuck out of there.

Chapter 14 – Ramona

There's a knock at the door and Ramona and Celina stop making out with each other. All ten people laughing and cheering get quiet—the Olympia beer cans hide behind bunk beds, chair legs, and bodies. Ramona feels tingly as she crosses the room—she likes making out with women, appreciating their beauty, and can't help but feel hot when everyone's watching her.

It could be the R.A. so she cracks the door carefully.

Good, it's just Nick—just dropping by. She loves it when people do that. His clean-shaven thin white face turns towards her and she reaches for his hand and leads him in.

His head bobs up and down at everyone, and then he stops still in the middle of the room. "A surprise party? For me?" he says, and gets a couple chuckles. This is *not* Nick's group—it's the activist crowd that Ramona hangs with. Someone yells "surpriiiiiiiiiiise" in a stoner voice, like ten seconds too late.

Ramona's stomach rises slightly—the last time Nick interacted with this group was at Celina's Saffron Revolution party when he ripped down her Jonas Brothers poster and went on a drunken tirade about boy bands and how she can't be a real activist and have a boy band poster. She told him that it's called irony and that the Jonas Brothers rock and that he must leave her house immediately. He told her she didn't own the house so he's not leaving. She told him she was going to call the cops. He told her he knew she was going to call the cops because she's a snitch and she loves the police and she loves the government. His friends carried him out.

But whatever—Nick ended up buying her a replacement poster that was a pop-up one and kicked ass.

Nick leans over into Ramona's ear. "Is this a party?"

"Sorta."

"A ceremony?" he says, eyebrows rising.

"Sorta," Ramona says. "Actually, it's just a game—like an adult Spin the Bottle. Sit down, you'll see." Ramona's learned that it's better to just give Nick clear directives.

"Okay," Celina says, directing her question to Ramona. "When you're eighty years old, who, in this room, would you like to spend the rest of your life with?"

"Oooooooo. Gooooood one," Melody says. Ramona stands and then rotates in quick little jerks, 360 degrees, giving each of the thirteen people their fair share of consideration. She pictures herself as an eighty year-old in a little log cabin in the woods, sitting in a wheel chair eating pancakes. And then she knows who she would choose, so she approaches Brian, Melody's boyfriend, gives him a little look, and then tips onto her toes, pecks his lips a couple times before opening her mouth on his and leading a convincing make-out session. His full, lumberjack beard parts ways for his big, pink lips and tongue, and Ramona tries to ignore the ash tray flavor of his mouth.

"Awwwwww, Monaaaaa. That's, like, *really* sweet," Melody says as she dips her chin down to her chest and drops the sides of her mouth. "You think Bri would be the best to spend your final days with." She sounds almost tearful with the compliment, and it makes Ramona want to run over and give her a hug, but instead she just shoots her friend a sincere air-kiss and returns to her spot.

Ramona turns to explain it to Nick. "So, since I was the one answering the question, I made out with the person I chose for my answer," she says. "And now I'm the one who asks the question… Get it? You'll see." She squints at Brian. "Hmmmmmmmmmm. Bri—Who would you breed with… besides Melody… to create the ultimate warrior to fight for the survival of the human race? Like, if the world was being taken over by zombies and your future child was the chosen one, who would you breed with to create that child?"

Brian hops out of his cross-legged position and walks up to Ramona. She furrows her brow—he can't choose the person who just chose him… and then, as he gets close to her, he suddenly spins to his left, where Nick is leaning against the post of the bunk bed, makes momentary eye contact with him, and then goes in for the kiss. Nick moves his head back an inch, but allows Brian to kiss him. He doesn't open his mouth, and after a few seconds Brian gets the message and stops. Everybody hoots and hollers in applause, and Nick has a nervous smile. "You're gonna breed with me, bro? Try that. I'd like to see you try that, and then watch what happens."

"Whoa! Toxic masculinity!" someone yells.

Nick's face is pink. You can almost see his heart bumping in his chest. "No—it's cool. It's cool. What's my question, dude?"

"Ummmmmm," Brian says. "Let's see. If you could copy off anyone in this room to pass a really big test, who would it be?"

"I wouldn't copy off anyone," Nick snaps back.

"No, I meant like," Brian says.

"Whose dick would you suck if I stuck it in your mouth?" Nick says, and the room erupts. Some are doing the "sssssssss" thing and a pillow comes flying down from the top bunk and misses Nick's head as he makes his way to the exit. Ramona follows him out of the room like she's a security guard protecting him from the paparazzi. She shouldn't have allowed him to play this game. Fuck—he's too offensive. He hasn't learned. No, he's learned, he just can't control himself. It's not okay. It's not okay to tell someone you'll put your dick in their mouth. Fuck. Why did she let him play?

He's fifteen feet in front of her and she calls his name.

"No. Fuck, every, single, person, in that room," Nick says, his cheeks looking like he just got socked on both sides.

"You need to control your temper—you cannot react that way over a guy kissing you. Seriously. I thought you were past that."

Nick stops—his eyes ricochet in all directions like he's searching for thoughts in the sky. "I swear to God, if that dude says anything to me again…"

"If it were a woman, would you have reacted the same way?" she says, carefully.

"That was not a woman—that was a big ass hairy man. And just 'cause he wears sandals and a sweater and fucks hippie chicks…" Nick shakes his hand from side to side. "He's a fucking dick."

He takes off down the sidewalk, his breath shooting smoke into the air. Whenever guys get mad, all of their sensitivity and political correctness go out the window. Nick suddenly stops and continues what he was saying. "You're a woman, I'm a man, right? I can't tell you how to be a woman and you can't tell me how to be a man. It's that simple."

She sees what Nick's saying—nobody can really understand someone else's experience. But it's *not* that simple. Guys have been running the show and making their own rules forever, and look how it's worked out for women? It is time for men to start listening to women's feedback on how they act.

"Do you really believe in this whole free love thing anyway?" Nick says, his temper cooling down.

"If it isn't free, can you really call it love at all?" Ramona says.

"Dude." Nick pauses and looks at her. "You know what I mean. Like against marriage and shit. Kids." He walks over to the wooden telephone pole and starts picking out a staple from a "Missing Dog" flyer.

"I definitely want kids. But without the whole marriage legalized prostitution thing." And she says this, thinking about what she's studied through anarchism about ownership and having control over people and how marriage is one of those things that helps men control and have possession over women and sex. And when she starts thinking about that, it all just makes her sick. At the same time she can't help but remember what her grandma told her when she was a little girl. About how marriage was like a fence that you put around a garden so it can grow to be beautiful. She always kind of liked that metaphor.

"So you don't have a problem walking in on your baby's dad fucking some bimbo in your bed while the baby's crying?" Nick says. He likes to challenge her anarchist ideas.

"Ummm," she says. "Number one, that just sounds like shitty parenting, and I hope I would have a child with someone more skilled at parenting. Number two, I hope he wouldn't be so shallow to be fucking a bimbo. And number three, why is he fucking in our bed?"

"Because there's no private property in anarchism," Nick says, proud of himself, three inches from her face.

"But there is personal property—remember you're allowed to have personal property, and I would call a bed personal property."

"What?!" Nick says. Ramona can tell that this is the first time Nick has heard this argument. "So I can have a 50 square mile mansion of personal property. Yeah right."

"No," Ramona says. "Because everyone in the world having a bed is completely feasible and everyone having a 50 mile mansion is horrible and impossible. How could you have a mansion with thirty extra rooms when there are homeless people? That affects their personal freedom so that goes against anarchism."

"There are people without beds, so that's affecting their personal freedom—you having a bed and not sharing," Nick counters.

"You could make that argument. It's a bullshit, weak one, but you can always make an argument about what limits people's personal freedom and what doesn't. But if people honestly thought about that and asked themselves that question when they made decisions, things would be a lot better."

"Whatever dude. I'm gonna catch this bus. Alex stole my truck again—I think he got a job delivering pizzas or something."

"Hey," she says, and walks towards him, wishing he wouldn't leave just yet. He turns around, and is looking in her direction but without making eye contact. She embraces him and pulls him to her. He doesn't return the hug, but doesn't push her away either. "I'm sorry that that happened."

"I'll talk to you later," he says, turning away from her and then turning back. "You have two dollars I could borrow?"

She gives him the money and he walks to the bus stop.

Chapter 15 – Quintavious

Q runs into T on his way out the door. "That's the man I'm trying to see!" Q says, then tells him he's on his way to meet Ramona by the lake.

"What y'all gonna do on the lake, have Eskimo sex?" T says in his smooth, slow voice, looking high as hell.

"Naw man, I don't know. She talkin' bout she want to walk around it or something."

"Damn, you whipped already? She got you doing laps around the lake? Mmmm, mmmm, mmm," T shakes his head and then cracks up.

"If I ain't gotta spend dough, it's cool with me. But ay, lemme get a little somethin somethin in case she wanna smoke." Quint reaches in his pocket and pulls out a money roll. He flips through it, even though he knows it's a hundred and fifty—his punk-ass boss didn't show up to pay him on Friday so he had to go the whole weekend on E, but now it means he's got a good chunk of change and it's only Tuesday.

"You ain't paid your mom yet?" T says, looking at Quint's money.

"Nigga who is you? Did I ask you to be my bank manager or did I ask you for some motherfucking trees? Shit…" Quint says, scrunching up his face. "Yeah I paid my mama."

He peels off a pink ten, gets a bag from T, and is on his way to meet Ramona by the picnic tables, like they decided, before walking around the lake. He had been nervous when he called her, but had a feeling she would be cool, unlike so many other girls; and he was right—she picked up and said she wasn't hungry but that she was dying to get out of the dorms and get some fresh air. Quint was kind of surprised about wanting to go on a walk in winter. He just always thought it was weird to walk without no type of destination, just to walk, but you can't argue with a woman on a first date.

It's forty degrees out so he's wearing his brother's black Timberlands, some khaki Carhartt pants, a black Girbaud sweater and his black jacket with the brown fur around the hood.

He walks east around the south side of the lake, looking at the surface of the water and how it's still frozen near the edge but has turned back to liquid in the middle. His breath hits the air and turns into steam. He wonders how it's going to be with Ramona—if she's going to be the same as when she's drinking or if it's going to be different and uncomfortable. She *is* a college girl… She might just make him feel stupid like some of them do. Like when they be talking about some shit and you just have no idea what they saying. Yeah, maybe it's a bad idea to go. Why risk it? But then there's that feeling when she's around. That feeling makes him finally able to forget. Or not forget, but be able to break through the pollution that has been sitting in his stomach since dad passed when he was ten. She's definitely got that thing about her. That thing he ain't felt in a while, and never felt with a white girl.

The question is, what is *she* doing? Why would she want to go out with him…

He's still about ten minutes away from the picnic tables when he looks up and sees her walking toward him with those acorn eyes and that smile like she did something bad. The pollution lifts out of his stomach and then his cheeks break into a smile. Her face looks fresh out of the shower—but that's the only part of her that's showing. She's got some kind of snow hat on that looks like ear-muffs and a hat mixed into one. And mittens, blue jeans and a green vest over a big brown sweater.

"I couldn't wait at the picnic tables. I needed to walk," Ramona says.

"I feel you. I can't stay inside like some people. If I watch TV for like two hours, I know I gotta take my behind outside or else I'ma end up fighting with someone in the house," he says. "I gotta be honest, though, if I walk, I gotta be walking somewhere."

She smiles. "That's how I feel when I play sports. Like, why am I running back and forth, chasing a little ball?" She gives him a quick hug. "But this is great! It's just nice to get out of that artificial heat and into the fresh air, you know?" They turn back and head to the east side of the lake.

"Yeah," he says. They walk along the path and Quint thinks of a question to ask her. "So I could tell you're a party girl—what'd you do after that beach party the other night?"

"Well I was looking for you," she smiles. "No—you've only seen one little embarrassing part of me. I'm actually not that much of a party girl, sorry to say. Not that I haven't had my party days. My parents actually sent me off to boarding school for high school—it was their way of, like, not having to raise me. So I did the college party girl thing in high school. And now I'm pretty much over it."

"Um hmm," Quint says. "I can tell."

"Whatever." She squints at him. "So what about Quintavious? You probably have the ladies knocking down your door. Is there someone special?"

Quint leans back like a pimp, "Well, I did meet this girl the other night, but then her stomach was acting up, right. And then I seen her again, at this party, right, where she was wearing a swim suit and little blue skirt; but I think she went home with the guy with the surf board."

Ramona starts laughing and bumps into him on purpose. "Oh no, so you had the pleasure of meeting Chris? What a tool, right? He's just a freshman, though, so you can't blame him too much. He's just a baby." Ramona walks out to the edge of the path, where there's a concrete ledge that drops down about three feet to where the lake starts. She looks back at Quint: "You think the ice would hold me if I walked out on it?"

"You must be crazy. It ain't nothing but a thin layer of ice," he says.

Ramona locks eyes with him and starts walking sideways to the edge. She steps down on the snow covered rocks and then onto the snow covered ice. She's trying to play with him but it's not funny. He takes out a Newport and sparks it.

"Come on! It's so thick. I can tell."

Quint's stomach rises into his chest—why is she playing like this? He turns around to go but then turns back around. He can't. It's only two feet deep where she's at, and she's only fucking around—don't let something so small ruin everything. What would a normal person do?

He drags his cigarette, then picks up a big chunk of wood from the other side of the path. He takes the timber back and then tosses it, over Ramona's head, and onto the lake surface ten feet in front of her—the piece punches through the snow and ice, revealing the dark water beneath it.

"Okay, okay, I believe you," Ramona says. She comes up the bank and joins him. He tries to give her a smile but it comes up short. She stands there, looking into his face and searching his expression, trying to figure it out what's behind it. He can tell she doesn't know, that she has no idea, and yet he's cool with her. It's like she's one hundred percent serious and one hundred percent concerned. It actually makes him feel good. Feel better. They keep walking.

Quint sees his homeboy Monte walking and says what's up. He wonders what Monte thinks about him walking with someone like Ramona, with a white girl. But not only that, she's a *University* girl. Monte probably doesn't give a fuck, though, and who the fuck is Monte anyway? Quint tells himself to stop trippin.

Ramona pulls out a film canister. She leans up to his face like she's going to tell him something really personal and then says, "umm, do you get stoned?" She lifts off the top of the film canister and lets him examine the contents. The strong, rich odor tingles inside his nose.

"Oohh-kay!" he says, "I knew I liked you for some reason! Just playin."

"I figured you probably smoked, but I didn't want to like, stereotype or anything," Ramona says.

"Oh, so you was gonna stereotype me—I see. So you thought all handsome, swagged out guys smoke weed?" Quint nudges into her a little bit, but is careful that his enormous frame doesn't knock her into the snow bank.

"Exactly," Ramona says with pursed lips.

Quint really begins to relax now. For some reason, just walking around the lake with no plan made him nervous. But now that there is an actual plan, that they're going to smoke, everything is cool. Now all he wonders is how they are going to smoke it. Every time he smokes with white people, they either smoke out of a glass pipe or a bong. The glass pipes seem weird—too close to a crack pipe—but he loves the bong. "You tryna get a blunt or you have something else in mind?"

"I don't know, we could. Or if you want to walk over to my room, my roommate is like a serious stoner and has this bubbler that will get you high in like one hit—it's ridiculous."

"Let's do it," Q says. Along the north side of the lake, Quint explains that the area used to be the hood, but now is all subdivisions and suburbs. "But the thing is, shit still go down on the north side. These little suburb kids be thuggin for real. I swear, it doesn't look like the ghetto, but it's almost just as bad."

They walk to the west side of the lake, by the picnic tables, and then Ramona leads them to her section of the dorms called the Veggie Co-op.

"So you live in the special dorms? Like for the smart kids, or the slow kids?" Q says, joking, even though they did put him in the slow class a couple times when he was in school.

"No, we all make a commitment to only eat vegetarian food in the building and once a month we have to cook for all thirty people who live there."

"Hmmm. I don't know if I could do all that," Quint says under his breath.

Ramona opens the door to the co-op and the smell of onions cooking in butter lights up the building. Quint's stomach opens up and his mouth gets moist but he doesn't say anything. They walk upstairs to Ramona's room, which is unlocked but nobody's there. Maybe they leave their rooms unlocked. There are pictures all over the walls, and everything seems to be either red or purple. Q tours the perimeter. She has pictures of friends, pictures of nature, pictures of her and her friends *in* nature. It's like you would think she lived in the woods by the beach on a mountain. No wonder she wanted to walk around the lake.

She reaches in a drawer by her roommate's bed and pulls out the big, dark red glass bubbler. Quint's seen something like it in stores, but he's definitely never smoked out of one. It's like a glass pipe with a big nut sack hanging down on the end, below the bowl. Ramona tells him she needs to change the water in it so she goes to the bathroom. Quint stands there. Alone. There's a picture of Ramona and a couple people standing around a ranger who is showing them a gigantic turtle. Wait—who is that ranger? Is that the cop? It looks like his ass. No—he's tripping. Gunshot blasts ricochet through his skull and he squints to squeeze them out. He needs to drink or smoke, fast.

The door finally unlatches and in she comes, holding the bubbler in front of her like a kid who just found an Easter egg. He breathes and it's like the air changes once she comes in—maybe he just needed her to come back. Even his insides change—it's like a warm shower is pouring over his cold body.

She retrieves a nugget, which seems almost furry with little orange and yellow hairs, and pulls it into two pieces. The bud is so sticky that once she pinches it apart, it stays in the squished shape from her fingers—hopefully it's dry enough to smoke. She puts in one of the chunks and hands the red glass to Quint to spark.

"All right," he says, smiling at the unique situation he's in.

Even though Quint's never smoked out of a bubbler before, he's a veteran smoker and knows to put his finger on the carb while he lights the bowl. He does it and inhales as the herb lights and the smoke travels down from the bowl, through the bubbling water, and then out the stem and into his lungs. He can barely tell if he's getting a hit it's so smooth, and then he exhales a cloud of smoke that almost fills the room, causing Ramona to grab her purple towel and put it under the door.

He slowly passes her the bowl, and she puts it up to her quick-moving lips, takes a hit, coughs a couple of times, and looks so high that he has to shake the thought that she has pink eye. They each hit it one more time and then the ash from the weed gets sucked into the water. They're high and don't even think about the other bud, much less Quint's dime bag of mids. Ramona gets up and puts on some Portis Head on her computer. Quint has never heard anything like it, and it trips him out a little bit. Then Ramona comes over to him and starts doing a dance that looks like she's a snake trying to hypnotize him, with her body slithering back and forth but her face staying in the same spot— her eyes and mouth wide open. Even though she is looking kind of sexy, Q is thinking damn, she's really crazy, when she bursts into a laugh, signaling that she's just fucking with him.

Quint starts singing Cee Lo: "Maybe you're craaaazzeeeee, maybe you're cra-zeeee," They both start laughing. Quint is noticing how Ramona's the only person he's ever seen that gets more amped up after she smokes. But he has to admit, he feels good and energetic too. Where'd them trees come from?

After sitting there, zoning into the music for a minute, Ramona breaks the silence. "I need to like, move, or do something— so I'm gonna kiss you, okay?"

"Okay," Quint says with a calm smile. That's some shit females can do that niggas just can't, he thinks. She gets off the bed and walks over to where Q's sitting, puts her hands on his face, and kisses him with a wet mouth—like it was watering for his lips. She straddles his legs and sits on his lap, and they carefully taste each other. It's nice to get past the differences and down to something that they both know. He likes how she feels.

She gets up and, just as quickly as she came over, she says, "okay, good, now I feel better," and goes over to her desk and picks up her Nalgene bottle and takes a drink of water and offers Quint some. He normally doesn't share cups, but takes it and drinks. It tastes good and helps his cotton-mouth. "Are you hungry?" she asks.

"I could always eat," he says.

"Okay, I'm gonna go whip something up. Stay here, kay?"

"I'll be here." Shit, her roommate better not come back—she'll probably come in and think there's a home invasion going on.

He sits there and pictures himself kissing her naked body. His dick gets hard and he wonders if they're going to have sex—damn that would feel good. He scans the wall of pictures again, noticing that it's mostly white but there are a few people that look mixed.

Ramona comes back with some tortillas with melted cheese and salsa on the side. "Do you like quesadillas?" she asks. "I probably should have asked you before I went down."

"Yeah, looks good." They eat the quesadillas and talk about how good they taste.

Then Ramona starts talking about the dairy industry and how fucked up it is. Why would you talk about that while you're eating some cheese?

Q tries to zone out but can't help but listen, and starts picturing chickens in tiny cages being injected with hormones—their claws growing around the bars. He finishes his quesadilla and drinks the brown apple juice Ramona gave him, and it tastes even better than the cheese quesadilla. "Damn, girl, you can cook!" he says.

"Oh this is nothing," she says, shaking her head with a scrunched-up face. "My mom is ridiculous. That's like the one thing we could do together when I was growing up, is cook. Everything else turned into a fight."

"I can't picture you fighting with nobody," he says.

"You'd be surprised," she says, and throws a few punches into the air, but it looks more like she's shaking those African shaker instruments than like she's in a fight. "No just kidding, I don't do real fights, but I did get in a lot of yelling fights with my mom when I was growing up. She would tick me off so much because she would just ignore anything that was ever wrong. Ahhhhh, I hated it! Like if I ever came to her to tell her that I was sleeping with a boy or anything, she would just change the subject and act like she didn't hear me. That's why she sent me off to summer camp for the whole summer and then sent me to boarding school for high school—she just didn't want to be a parent."

"That's the opposite of my mama. She always trying to get in my grill, talking about, what's going on? Where you been? Who you chillin' with? That shit get on my nerves sometimes, but that's just my mama—she can't help it."

"I wish my mom was like that," she says. Then she walks towards him with her chin down and her eyes looking up at his. She's joking around, but he knows that even she knows she looks sexy. She kisses him and he tastes the sweet apple juice on her mouth. He gets up and walks her back over to her bed, kissing her along the way. She pulls him down on the bed. The music has somehow switched to Sade, and he wonders if she planned it like that.

They kiss and pull each other and escape into the feeling of attraction. She takes deep breaths and it turns him on. She presses her thigh into his erection.

He looks at her white skin on his brown skin and starts wondering if she's ever been with a black guy. She probably hasn't. He's only been with one white girl before, and she was a hood white girl and they were drunk as hell.

His hands are sweaty. What is she thinking? Is she nervous? Is she scared? Is she just pretending to be into it? Suddenly his dick isn't hard anymore. Instead, it seems to be taking a nap, cuddled up against his nuts like a sleeping caterpillar. Just relax and enjoy her. He takes a second to tilt his head back and just look at how sexy she is. He starts kissing her again and feels himself come back to life. He thinks about her pussy to help him stay up. "You want to? You know?" he says. He doesn't think he's ever asked this before. Usually he just goes with the flow and if a girl doesn't want to, then she tells him.

"Do you?"

"Yeah."

"Okay," she says. "So do I. Do you have a condom?"

"Yeah, I think I do in my wallet." He knows he does, but doesn't want to act like he was expecting to fuck. They continue rolling around on the bed. He takes off her shirt, and then she goes over to lock the door. She gets a drink of water and gives him some, and then comes back and starts kissing him and taking off his shirt at the same time. She takes off her bra and he feels her small breasts in his hands. Her whole body is small, skinny, and it makes him feel like a giant. She takes his dick out and rubs it with her hand— the grip of her warm fingers feels good. She pulls off his pants and as she passes his dick, gives it one kiss and looks up at him and smiles. He slowly tugs her pants all the way down to her ankles and then cuffs the bunched up jeans over her heels, freeing her legs. He kisses her shins and the inside of her knee. She takes a deep breath, which must be a sign that she's ready, so he feels for his pants on the floor, gets the condom out, and puts it on. He reaches down with his right hand and lifts his middle finger inside of her and feels her wetness, and then uses his other finger to help spread the lips and puts himself inside of her. She lowers herself onto him, adjusting slowly, until they are entirely connected. He pulls her body close and she starts moving her hips on him. It feels good. She keeps on rocking and tells him he feels good. He wonders what else she's thinking. Does she really like being with this big black guy? What does she want him to do? He continues to move with her, but it is almost like he is watching her and not participating. She keeps on moving but he realizes that his dick is going soft. He closes his eyes and tries to concentrate on getting hard, but it's not working. He decides to picture a black girl and starts quickening his thrusts, but he's in a halfway point between being hard and soft and he's trying to figure out if he's getting harder or softer—trying to figure out what she is thinking about—trying to picture Shawnese. As the questions blend together and ricochet against each other, his body answers him and his dick is definitely soft. "Are you okay?" Ramona asks, finally noticing.

"Yeah, I don't know what's going on, to be honest."

"Is it something I did?"

"I don't know what it is," he says as he pulls out, the condom baggy on his limp penis. "I ain't never had this happen before. I mean, it ain't you though, don't worry about that."

"It's okay, we probably shouldn't have had sex this quickly anyway," she says.

"My fault. I don't know what the hell is going on."

Chapter 16 – Marcus

"I'm taking a fifteen minute smoke break," Nick says.

"You said you didn't have cigarettes," Marcus says.

"I don't have cigarettes. That's why it's a *fifteen minute* smoke break, bro. Read between the lines."

"Oh I need a break too—I got a Swisher," says Marcus.

"Hurry up then," Nick says.

"You better clock out," Charles says.

Marcus will smoke with anyone, and Nick seems cool for a white boy. It's still hard to tell, but like, the good thing is that he stands for something—he's got his ideas and opinions about shit.

He doesn't just say what he thinks he *should* say—those are the motherfuckers Marcus really can't stand.

He gives Nick the cigar as they walk onto Patriot Boulevard to look for a spot. It's cold and dry, and the street is full of Friday afternoon traffic. "How about up here? You can't make it up?" Marcus says, pointing to a seven foot brick fence separating the sidewalk from the YMCA.

"What if Gary drives by?" Nick says.

"Bruh, stop being scary. It's Friday afternoon—I bet you he's gone for the weekend."

"Right on." Nick holds the Swisher in his mouth like a dog bone as he takes two steps and then springs, lifting his body easily to a sitting position. Impressive but not *too* impressive. Marcus runs straight *at* and then *up* the wall, popping up next to Nick, showing him how a real G does it.

"You need me to roll for you?" Marcus says.

Nick scrunches his face. "Who doesn't know how to roll a blunt?"

"Shit. Most white people, I bet you."

"No, bro. It's 2009—you can't graduate high school without knowing how to roll." Nick splits the cigar, empties the guts, licks the inside of the paper, fills it and smoothly reseals it. He hits it a couple times before passing it.

Marcus is about to hit it when a police car drives by. Normally he wouldn't even hesitate because it's too far away and police don't stop their cars for motherfuckers smoking, but it almost looks like *the* cop. It's hard to tell with the glare. Marcus leans forward.

"Hide that!" Nick says, and turns his head the other way.

"Bruh, why are you so paranoid?" White boys is *scary*—he got nothing to worry about. Marcus takes a long drag with his right hand. With his left, he lifts his arm and gestures a sniper rifle following the movement of the cop. "Nothing but target practice…" he says, and imagines the cop being the purple-lipped murderer and Marcus's hollow tipped bullets spreading on impact through the cop's skin and organs.

"No, I thought it was…" Nick hesitates. "Never mind," he says. "But bro, you can never tell if someone is a good cop or a bad cop. There are some dangerous situations that…"

"Bruh can you not start talking about this, bruh?" Marcus interrupts. "Like this will really ruin my high. Like, I actually study this shit on my free time, bruh, so you can't win this argument. You know where the police came from, right?" He smokes again, then passes it.

"What are you talking about, came from?"

"Police came from the slave patrols, bruh, that used to go around and snatch up all the slaves that escaped. The slave patrols, the KKK and the police is all the same group, bruh. So don't talk about a good cop, that's like being a good Nazi, bruh. Unless you a crooked cop, like a spy motherfucker that's really working to fuck shit up on the inside, it ain't no good cop."

"Bro. We need some police," Nick says as he holds in a hit. "You can't have gangs running the street, robbing people."

"What do you think the police is? They a gang that runs the street." Then Marcus starts thinking about *do they rob people.* "They don't rob people—they just shoot people. And capture people. And then, matter of fact, then they rob people. They rob your freedom. And once they got you locked up, they for sure take your shit. You ever been locked up? All them court fees, probation fees. Shit. All them bullshit tickets in general is robbery if you really think about it. Shit, they robbing the poor."

"What if someone in your family was a cop?" Nick asks.

"No one in my family would become a cop," Marcus says, and stares blankly at the sidewalk below as he takes a long pull. He feels the smoke expand his chest. "Trust me." Why would Nick ask that question? Maybe he should really just lace him with the whole truth about his dad's murder and see how he responds. But he doesn't feel like going there, especially right before going back to work. "Bruh, remind me never to smoke with your ass again. You really try to kill a motherfucker's high, don't you?"

Nick smiles with glazed eyes. "You're just a beginner; you'll learn to smoke through that."

"You stupid," Marcus laughs. "Hurry up and smoke or pass, then, if you such a veteran. We gotta get back and clock in."

Nick pulls out some Visine and drops the back of his head and squeezes a few drips in each eye ball. *So that's how white boys hold onto their jobs...* The only time Marcus used eye drops was with his grandma—after she had her cataracts surgery. She had three different drops she had to take every few hours, so she would move from her recliner to the kitchen chair, tilt her head back and strain to get her eyes pointed towards her forehead. He liked doing that for her—he liked how she trusted him to take care of her.

Marcus takes the little clear bottle and imitates Nick, then pulls out his own spray deodorant. The two of them smell like artificial flower as they walk into the parking lot of the sign shop.

Then they stop in the middle of the lot.

Fuck. Gary's Expedition is parked next to a patrol car. A fucking patrol car. Hell no… Gary was supposed to be gone for the weekend and what is the police doing here? Should he still go in? He's gotta go in. He looks over and this dude Nick is dipping out the parking lot like he's wanted by the police! Maybe he *is* wanted by the police. Is that the reason they're here? Damn, this type of shit always happen when you smoke.

Marcus enters the shop and it feels like it's a hundred degrees in there. The cop has his back toward him, talking to Gary, but then he turns. Not all the way around, but far enough so that Marcus can see him.

Recognize him.

The purple lips.

Shots blast in his head while he watches the purple lips move. His dad mowing the lawn. Little Quint laying tased by the gate. It's too much noise and just when he thinks his body is going to give out, overheat, pass out, it suddenly steadies itself. It does what it always does, and he knows this about himself. That's how you have to be in high stress situations—calm and cool.

He reaches up to Charles's face and removes the glasses from his stepdad. "It's *him*."

"You play too much—give me my…" Charles says.

"STOP!" Marcus interrupts. "You not hearing me, bruh. That's the cop that killed Dad, *bruh*."

Charles doesn't say anything. What can he say? It's certain things you can say to certain people, and this is one of those areas where Charles knows he can't say shit. When it comes to Marcus's real dad, their whole relationship changes. From *step-dad-and-step-son* to *step-out-the-way-because-you-have-no-idea*.

"What you need my glasses for?" he finally says.

Marcus sucks in his stomach, hikes his baggy khakis above his belly button, stuffs his red work polo into them, and then re-fastens his belt on the tightest notch. He locates a blank work order, clipboard, pen, and blade.

"Ay," Charles says, commanding attention. "You need to stay your ass back here. Your mom wouldn't want…"

"You say Mom one more time." Marcus puts the spectacles on and everything is blurry and soft like he's underwater. He bobs to the doorway leading to the front area and then stops. He hears them. One more step and he'll see them. They'll see him. One more step and there's no turning back. He stands there, listening.

Gary is talking to the cop. "Nick? Nick Nelson? Why? You can take him. Is he a criminal too? God damn, seems like all my guys have been in the slammer." *So that's why Nick bolted—they are looking for him.* Marcus peeks around the doorway.

The cop looks down, pauses, and then says, "No, he's not in trouble. I just wanted to check up on him."

"Anything we can do, let me know. We sure appreciate the work you do—I know it's not easy trying to keep this city under control," Gary says, beaming in front of him like he wants an autograph. Marcus tilts his blurry glasses up to review the work order. He reaches in his pocket and rubs his sweaty fingers over the brail-like grip of the X-acto knife handle.

"I tell ya…" the cop says. "Other night I get a homicide call. Go out there, and the shooter had shot the transformer out with a shotgun. Whole block lost electricity, shooter goes free," the cop says.

Marcus is motionless, breathing through his mouth. He peeks over at the Glock in its holster and wonders how new it is. How often do they replace those guns? Could it be the same one as ten years ago? Marcus twists off the plastic guard on the blade in his pocket and rubs the razer point with his finger.

"They get too many chances if you ask me," Gary says. "How about one strike and you're out, then they'll think twice."

"We would if we could, but the jails are clogged. So we get as many as we can—put the rest on probation," he laughs.

"Well how can we help you today?"

"I need a banner for a community barbeque we're doing." He reaches into a folder and pulls out a couple images. "We want this police picture on the bottom and then we want this picture of the family on top, like we're lifting up the family."

"Good afternoon, gentlemen! Mr. Officer," Marcus says, springing on the scene. "May I finish off this work order and get it started? What do we say?"

Gary looks at Marcus like what the hell are you doing, and is about to open his mouth, when the purple-mouthed cop speaks. "That sounds great. I like this guy, Gary! See, you're doing good work, giving opportunities to these guys." He stands, wide-mouthed, reflecting Marcus's grin. Marcus is glad that he's wearing the blurry glasses and restrains his hands from squeezing the cop's neck until there is no life.

"Fantastic!" Marcus says, and lifts his hand for a high five. The cop hesitates, and then touches hands. "Let's finish up the specs for the sign and then jot down a contact phone and address and I'll get right on it."

The cop points at Marcus with his thumb. "I'll be damned—where'd you get this guy? He's good—knows how to speak and everything."

"He's new," Gary grunts, and then lifts his eyebrows at Marcus. Marcus ignores him. "Still on probation."

"He's a keeper!" the cop says, and tells Marcus his name, phone number and address. He shows Marcus the pictures he wants to use. "So the basic idea," he starts to explain, "is that the police are lifting and protecting the community so that families stay safe. And really thrive with whatever it is they're trying to do. We want people to see officers as members of their own team," he says. "What do you think of that?"

"Protecting the family… we can do that." Marcus shoves his hands into his pockets to prevent his fists from flying. His right hand bounces back out, fingers gripping a thread of bright red.

"Jesus Christ, son, you're bleeding," the cop says.

"Allow me to return to my workstation and Mr. Gary Sir will finish the transaction," Marcus spits the words through his clenched jaw.

He walks straight to the bathroom with his left hand cupping the blood from his right fist. *1060 Panorama Drive.* He memorizes it.

Breathe, he reminds himself.

Chapter 17 – Quintavious

"Wow," Ramona says, sweaty and breathing hard. "That was. Like. Really. Good." Her small breasts rise and descend with each breath. Quint lies there too—his big hand next to her small stomach. But he's happy. And most of all, relieved; relieved that he redeemed himself from that first encounter. It helps when you're not so high and scatter-brained that your dick forgets it's in a pussy and goes limp during every non-sexual thought that enters your head. This time he was just happy to be with Ramona—everything just flowed. He liked talking to her, he liked kissing her, and he liked having sex with her.

He leans over and kisses her next to her eye. She kisses his ear, laughs, and then goes to the bathroom. Girls always be doing that after sex.

She comes back and puts her head on Quint's lap. He's checking out shoes in the East Bay catalog. Drama and Dora see that the door isn't latched and poke their snouts in to open it. They wiggle their bodies and wag their tails as they say hi.

"Look at the sweet pet bulls," Ramona says in baby voice. "What a sweet pet bull you are, Dora. Yes you are. Hello, Drama, yes, you're sweet too." The triangle heads and chunky bodies bump into each other as they position themselves for pets.

"Pit bulls. It's *Pit* bulls," Quint says.

"Look at the little *pet* bulls. Look at the little muscular bodies. I love the muscular bodies. Yes, Drama, you're going to be a famous Shakespearian actress 'cause your name's Drama! Yes you are," Ramona says. She turns back to Q. "I was up all night working on a paper on Ebonics—about whether it should be recognized as a language in schools. I seriously only slept like one hour."

"You wrote about Ebonics?" Quint says. What's she know about Ebonics? Is she like obsessed with black people or something? "What did you say? You think it's like a whole different language even though it use basically the same words as regular English?"

"Well the research shows that it has enough similarities to African dialects to be considered its own language." Ramona scrunches her eyebrows and makes her eyes really big. "So I think people who speak it would be better respected if it was acknowledged."

"I don't know about that." He thinks about it. "What about a doctor, what's he look like speaking in Ebonics?" Quint says.

"Well if they have patients who speak Ebonics, it's helpful. I think the goal is to be bilingual. And what I found was that schools would get more money because they would get more ESL funding from the government. And the teachers would also get training on how to teach academic English while respecting Ebonics."

"That's crazy," Quint says, his whole head still in thought. "That's why I love chilling with you, 'cause it be like you know some shit about my life that I don't even know. But actually I already know it, but I just ain't thought about it in that way before. You know what I'm saying?"

"Totally."

"And you know what I just thought about. Like, if you're black and you talk too square, like you're too smart, everybody think you a sellout, like you sound white. Like black people can't be smart or else they acting white. But like, if Ebonics is allowed, maybe brothas won't think you a sellout just 'cause you smart."

"I'll have to put that in my paper," Ramona says. "Don't worry, I'll give you a footnote."

Quint looks down at her and smiles. Should he ask her what a footnote is? Naw. "So you're just using me for my ghetto perspective?"

Ramona's eyes light up. "Yep, pretty much! Ghetto perspective and that sexy smile." She sticks her face three inches from his. "I just wanna take that smile and roll it into a little ball and stick it in my pocket!"

"I'ma roll you in a little ball and stick you in my pocket," Quint says.

"I'ma roll you in a little ball, dip you in some powdered sugar and pop you in my mouth!"

"I'll roll you in a lil ball, put you in the oven for about fifteen minutes, take you out, put some frosting on you, then put some sprinkles on you, and then pop you in my mouth!" Q says back and gives a little squeeze to Ramona's belly.

"I'm gonna roll you in a ball, put some butter and garlic on you, stick you in the toaster oven for three minutes, then eat you up!" Ramona says, laughing, while holding Quint's jaw in her hand and kissing his lips.

"I'ma roll you in a ball, drop you in some pickle juice for abouououout five days,"

"Pickle juice!"

"Yep," Q says, but before he can finish he hears the front door open and then, "Ay, Quint! Quint!" Marcus shouts and then the front door slams.

"Yeah! The fuck you want?" Quint yells, shaking his head. He turns to Ramona. "That's him right there." Marcus's rapping fills the house.

"Unsafe and unscared, nigga, that's the life/
Try and stop me, nigga, it'll be your life/
It'll be your wife/
Then it'll be your kid/
Try me and it's *bad*, like a 50 year bid."

"Shut your lame ass up," Quint says as Marcus walks in, hand all bandaged up and his arm in plastic wrap.

"Tat, tat, tatted up, tat, tat, tatted up! Check it out!" Marcus says, doing a little dance. Suddenly he sees Ramona and stops. Stares.

"Hey," she says.

"What the hell you get, man?" Quint says, smiling and looking at the ink on Marcus's arms. "Okay! Okay! What's that say?"

"This my new shit right here, bruh!" He tilts his forearms and pulls the Saran wrap snug so Quint can read the lettering. It says, UNSAFE down his right forearm and UNSCARED down his left in big wide letters. "Nigga we living in a unsafe world and you gotta be unscared in this bitch. I was walking home last night, right, past them big-ass houses, and I was thinking they safe, maybe, but they scared—and then I was thinking damn, that's what motherfuckers is—they either safe and scared or they unsafe and unscared—and nigga, if it's one thing I could say for my life, I say I rather be unsafe and unscared than safe and scared. So I said fuck it, got my check today and threw that whole thing on some ink, my nigga." He lets it sink in for a few seconds and then remembers Ramona, "Who that is?" he cocks his head towards her but keeps his eyes on Quint.

"Oh my bad, this is Ramona," Q says.

"She the police?" Marcus says, finally looking at her, up and down.

"Nigga shut that shit up. This the girl I was telling you about."

"Probably is the police. Mama know she in the house?"

"I'm a grown ass man," Quint starts, and then realizes that he's explaining himself to his little ass brother. "Does Mama know you in here? Why don't you call her and ask her what you need to be doing, 'cause this is a grown folks room in here."

"Riiiiight. Grown folks. Good luck with that. Don't be surprised if she got a wire on her," Marcus says as he exits, then starts rapping. "You know we keep that white girl—Christina Aguilera/ My jewelry's too loud, homeboy, I can't hear ya."

Quint flexes his tongue against the back of his teeth—his big cheeks twitch. Ramona doesn't say anything, but scoots away from him and then starts gathering her things. Fuck—she's not putting up with that shit and is about to leave. He should really teach that little motherfucker a lesson. He should just beat his ass right now, right in front of Ramona. Actually, what is he even talking about? Why would he let his little brother get to him like this? Get him this mad? He's breathing hard, and there's a weird way in which he likes the feeling. This strong feeling. There's a certain part of him that's amused by it. By this. It's different. Something's finally breaking through. Like taking off layers of jackets and feeling the wind on his skin. Because it's *something*. At least he's feeling *something*. And he's not even drunk or high.

Ramona steals his attention—she's putting on her boots. Probably it's best to just let her go. If she's really gonna be this sensitive to Marcus… You can't take some white chick over blood. And what is he doing catching so many feelings for a female anyway? It's not gonna work out—they from two whole different worlds.

"Bye," she says. Dressed, and ready to go. She has that look that tells him that if he doesn't say shit now, she ain't coming back. All he wants to do is stay quiet, let her stand there, shake her head, and then walk out the door forever.

But he can't.

He can't continue his life like this. He's got to do something. Mind over matter.

"Hold up. Hold up," he says. He walks over to her and holds her. She doesn't lean into him all the way, but lets him hold her as she stands upright. "I'm sorry. Don't worry about his lil lame ass—he think the whole world revolve around him."

His arms are like an inner tube around her, and she feels both tender and strong in his embrace. And it's true, Marcus is on some bullshit right now. And he actually respects Ramona for standing up to, or not standing for, that bullshit.

He holds her and is even a little bit proud of himself for the decision he made, because it isn't like him. Ten times out of ten he would have let her go. And even though he's shaking like crazy on the inside, he feels good that he finally took a chance, and on something positive—not just saying fuck it like he's been doing since he was eleven.

He keeps holding her for minutes, and tries to think if he's ever held a hug with someone for that long. Maybe his mom.

"I'm not okay with that energy," Ramona says.

"I feel you," he says. "The thing is, if you guys knew each other, like actually knew each other, then you would probably get along. Both y'all are into that whole save the world stuff—the revolution, stand up for your rights and shit. Only thing is he's more like run up on the government style and you more about peace."

"Yeah, sort of," Ramona says quietly. She's leaning back on Quint's lap, drawing squiggly lines on his arm with her finger. "I'm not just about peace though. I advocate anarchism."

"You what, who?"

"I advocate anarchism. That's what I believe in and work towards—anarchism."

"Like anarchy? Like no rules—where people can just wile' out and do whatever the fuck they want?" She really is on some shit.

"Not no rules—no hierarchy—no one above anyone else. Actual equality. What about you? What are you all about?"

Quint takes a deep breath. "I don't even know. I'm just like you don't fuck with me, I don't fuck with you. Don't hate on me getting mine and I won't hate on you getting yours, you feel me?"

"You're an anarchist," Ramona says and tips on her toes and gives him a peck on the lips. Quint squints his eyes and looks at her. "Yep," she continues. "Protecting people's personal autonomy. Everyone has the right to have personal freedom and as long as what they're doing doesn't impede on someone else getting theirs,'" she nudges him, "then nobody can tell them what to do."

"So my little brother can't hate on something that doesn't hurt nobody else, like what we do."

"If we're not harming anyone's personal freedom."

"I'm not harming anyone," Quint says and kisses her.

"That's sexy when you don't harm anyone," Ramona says in a breathy voice as she latches onto his mouth and then drags her tongue off his lip. Quint's belly bounces as he laughs. And then he thinks about his brother. About how Marcus really seems to hate white people. Like way more than he does. And *he* was the one who got tased by the white cop and made Dad get killed; but for some reason, he doesn't really trip off race like that, and Marcus judges everybody. Maybe it was the white Catholic school that Mom sent Marcus to. If Quint had been the one with the good grades and Mom had sent him there, would he feel the same about dating Ramona? Would he be like Marcus? Does Marcus know something he doesn't know?

Quint feels like the silence is getting awkward and wants to say something, but he doesn't want to talk about anything he's thinking so he stays quiet until Ramona says something.

"Hey," she says. "How many people have you had sex with?"

"Why you wanna know?" Quint says with his signature smile.

"Just tell me," she sighs. "It's harder to talk about this stuff later on in relationships."

"So we in a relationship?"

"We relate, don't we?" she says.

"You always got something different to say, don't you?"

"I see relationships as what you have with everyone you interact with."

"Here we go."

"I didn't say we were in an exclusive relationship." Wait, so is she messing around with other dudes? Whatever—she could if she wants. "Can you answer my original question about fucking please?" she says. Q smiles and shakes his head.

"How many dudes you had sex with?" he says.

"Asked you first," she says with her quick little mouth before he even finishes his question.

"You know, about average, I'd say. Not too many. But, you know, enough," he says, honestly, he thinks.

"Two? A hundred? Is there a number or is it too many to count?"

"Naw. I'd say like, probably, about fifteen."

"Oh… Okay," she says and lays her head on his chest like the conversation is over.

"And??" he says. "You just gonna ask a question and then not answer it?"

"Oh… Meeeeee, twenty-two."

"God damn!" he says.

"What? That's not a lot. I'm twenty years old so it's an average of one person a year, with a remainder of two."

Quint wrinkles his forehead. "But you don't have sex till you at least thirteen or fourteen."

"I thought it was like seventeen or eighteen," Ramona says. She explains how she went to a boarding high school and it was like living in the college dorms, with everyone fucking everyone.

"So everybody was some freaks?" he says. Ain't that some shit. White people really do get to live the life.

"Umm, kind of," she says. "But actually, I see sex kind of like, there's *touching*," she pauses, "and then there's touching *again*. I've *touched* many, but I've only touched *again* a select few."

"I see what you mean—you don't really fuck dudes more than once."

"Men and women. Well, not unless I like you," she says, and looks up at Q.

Quint presses his tongue to the inside of his cheek and shifts his jaw—did she count their first failed attempt as an actual time? "What kind of freaky stuff you did?"

She looks around with a half smile—she's definitely thinking of something.

"What'd you do, you little freak?" Q says, smiling. He notices that he's not being judgmental at all. Like he really doesn't care what she did. Maybe it's because they just started messing with each other. Kind of like what Ramona was saying.

"Nothing really. When I was a senior, I was at a party and these three poor little freshmen were talking about what it would be like to get a blow job and I just felt bad for them so I ordered them in a room, told them each where to stand, made them strip all their clothes off, and gave them each a blow job. Two of them came in like thirty seconds and the other one was too nervous to get an erection. And then after that, people wanted to give me a reputation, but they couldn't really figure out what category of reputation it fell in. The only one that stuck was the ninth graders referring to me as the sex therapist."

"Damn," Quint says, smiling. "The sex therapist?"

"What's the most outlandish sexual experience you've had?" Ramona asks.

"Who me?" Quint looks around the room. "I'm pretty old school when it come to all that freaky stuff. Let me see… All's I really did was have sex in the bathroom at East Side High—but e'rybody did that."

"Oooo, that doesn't sound very romantic. Or sanitary."

"Oh. It was this other time. Me and Marcus and my other homeboy was making a porno with this one chick, right?"

"Oh my god."

"And then my mama walk in and the girl hides behind the door, right? So my mama come in and see three niggas butt naked with a camera. She like, 'what the fuck?' Then finally she see the girl and relax a little bit. But she was still mad though."

"Whoa," Ramona says. "I guess I asked the question so I can't get mad at the answer." They move to the bed and Ramona curls her body into Q.

He turns on the TV and switches channels until it's at Family Feud. The question is "What are five things you shouldn't do in someone else's car?" There's one slot left and Ramona sleepily guesses "throw-up" and Quint guesses "ride dirty." The number five slot flips and shows "Vomit" and Q looks over to see why Ramona isn't celebrating. She's passed out, deep in sleep.

He's not tired yet so he takes a shower. As he's washing himself he thinks about Ramona and how he likes that she just does her thing and lets him do his.

"I like a independent girl that I can sleep next to/
Wake up in the night, I can make sweet sex to/
One that I can be myself, never have to flex to/
Skip one night of pussy and she'll focus on the next two."

Quint tells himself to remember the rhyme because he wants to write it down, but he forgets about it by the time he gets out of the shower. He dries off, puts on deodorant, touches up his hairline with some clippers, and then walks back into his room, gets in bed next to Ramona and falls asleep.

Chapter 18 – Marcus

"What the fuck, bruh? Now they got T? My nigga's gonna be locked up for more than a year over two goddamn rocks? Fuck that," Marcus says, clenching his teeth together. Psycho and Kenny stand there, straight faced, eyebrows high. "That don't make no sense, bruh. He didn't do nothing to nobody. I mean, he ain't hurt nobody. And now my nigga's locked up for a year! We can't just let these crackers get whoever the fuck they want." Marcus faces Kenny and Psycho and shakes his head back and forth.

"That's the way it is. My nigga's doing some time. He'll be back," Psycho says, and gleeks some spit onto the ground.

"No, bruh," Marcus says, closing his eyes. "I'm not gonna let this shit happen." He keeps his eyes closed and thinks about T and how he's known him since Kindergarten. Why do they do this? If they knew T, they wouldn't do this. He ain't no threat to nobody. They just killed his dreams. He wanted to be a P.E. teacher or a coach, and now he ain't gonna be able to do either one. "He just making that god damn paper and then they gon' go lock him up so he can't be there for his mufuckin son—and the cycle continues, bruh, I swear to god. Give me that bottle, my nigga, let me hit that one time."

Lil Kenny nods his chin at the bottle of Seagram's and Marcus passes him the bumpy glass. Psycho is just standing next to them, soaking in what everybody is saying—his breathing is hard and he looks like he could flip any second.

"I need some food, bruh. I ain't ate all day," says Kenny.

"Get you a slice of pizza," says Marcus. "And get me one too. I give you some money tomorrow when I get paid."

"I ain't got no more money, nigga, you know that. I bought this bottle."

"We gettin pizza," Psycho says, like it's the final decision. "Come on." Kenny and Marcus follow him to the payphone across the park. Psycho grabs the yellow pages attached to the phone booth and shakes it around until the top is facing up. He flips to the Ps and starts ripping out pages and throwing them on the ground until he comes to the pizza section. "Gimme fifty cents, bruh," he says to Marcus. Marcus gets fifty cents out of his pocket. He puts the money in the phone and dials a number. "Umm, I'm David… Yeah, let me get that five, five, five deal." He turns to Marcus and Kenny. "What y'all want? Okay, one pepperoni, one cheese, and one pepperoni with pineapples. And a two-liter of Coke. Yeah. We're at the University dorms, I'm on my way back there right now. From class." Marcus and Kenny look at each other, since it is actually Sunday. "My cell phone ran out of power so I'm at a pay phone," Psycho continues. He covers the phone and whispers, "what's the name of a dorm building?"

"Just say the new dorm, the one they just built."

"I'm in the new dorm… Oh, he could call 655-4420 but I might already be outside… Okay… Bye," Psycho says. "We getting some pizza, my nigga. We gonna break this cracker in two, my nigga!"

"They got cameras over there," Kenny says.

"Bruh, is you hungry or what? Stop being a little bitch-made nigga—is you hungry?"

Kenny looks at Marcus, wondering what he thinks.

"We gonna do this one for T," Marcus says. "They get one of ours, we get one of theirs." Psycho nods his head, happy that Marcus took his side. "That's what's holding mufuckas back. Niggas don't do shit. All we killin is our own. Niggas gotta stop being scared of the other side." Marcus tightens his belt and the other two follow suit.

They finish the bottle and walk to the new dorm to scope it out. It's got double glass doors and then a little office with a student worker inside. They talk about the plan and decide that Kenny is the smallest and looks the squarest so he'll be the one standing out there when the pizza comes. After about ten minutes of walking up and down the block, they see the pizza boy driving up in a blue pickup, so they walk over to their positions. Kenny waits with his back to the camera and Psycho and Marcus sit on the bench with their heads down, talking to each other.

The white pizza dude walks up with the three pizzas and a two-liter of Coke. He looks like he's about twenty-four—about six feet tall with dark hair. He looks up at Kenny and says, "Three pizzas and a Coke for David? Twenty one twenty five."

"Yeah. You got change for two twenties?" Kenny says.

"Nope. Just give me twenty bucks," the boy says, shaking his head and bouncing his shoulders. Marcus slowly gets in position. "If the pimp gets mad over a buck twenty five then he can try to call my bluff. He's got us working like hookers—working for pennies." What's this dude talking about? There's something strange, like he's almost too comfortable. You don't see white boys talking like that. "And what I told him was that I'd give him one more week to improve the working conditions," he continues, "and if he doesn't, then I'm unionizing Pizza Hut. The workers have the power and all you have to do is…"

Marcus's fist is in flight and comes crashing down on the boy's face. He absorbs the hit and stumbles back, trying to make sense of it all. "You're assaulting me?" is all he says before Psycho comes in with all his weight and socks him in the nose, sending him airborne. The boy lands on his back and blood starts flowing out of his nose like a water fountain. The two-liter falls to the brick patio and rolls ten feet and settles by the bench.

"Now, what? Cracker-ass bitch!" Psycho kicks him in the face and he curls into the fetal position. Marcus is booting him in the back and Kenny, even though he's holding three pizzas, is kicking him in the leg just so he can say he got some licks in. Some college students are screaming from the street and Marcus looks into the office and sees that the boy in there is on the phone.

"We out," Marcus says, and runs around to the dark side of the building. Kenny is right behind him, trying to run with the three pizzas in his hands. Psycho gets in one more kick and then joins them. Kenny hands off a box to each, and they continue running. Marcus grips his box with his arm around the side like a running back, Kenny holds his in front of him like he's a waiter, and Psycho holds his sideways in one hand—two pieces of cheese slipping out the bottom. They cut through alleys until they get to Kenny's backyard and rest on the back steps. They catch their breath as they open the come-up.

"I boxed that motherfucker's jaw like, uhhhhh!" Marcus says, acting out the replay, sweat sparkling on his face. His smile sputters on and off.

"You see me though, nigga, right in the nose like bam! Made that nigga leak. But I did get that cracker's blood on my shoe, punk ass bitch," Psycho says. They drink water from the hose and eat the pizzas, trying to laugh and feel good about everything.

"Ay, bruh, I don't think he was all the way with it. Like, didn't he seem a little off to y'all?" Kenny says.

"He was talking about *some* shit… I don't even know—all I know is I lit that nigga up!" Marcus says with a fake laugh.

Chapter 19 – Nick

Nick gets back from seeing his brother in the ICU and goes to the bar. He hasn't done this before—go to the bar, or turn to drinking—to get his mind off something. In fact, he was the one who always told his friends that that's when you know you're an alcoholic—when you stop drinking for fun and start drinking to feel better.

But tonight, fuck it—what's the other option, go to sleep? Yeah, right. He'd just lie there, picturing Alex's pasty white skin with crusts of scabby brown blood. And then the expression he had. The face of someone who had just tried for the very last time. It just doesn't make sense. Why Alex? He's barely hanging on, and finally listens to Mom and gets enough courage to get a job and actually go out and start working.

Nick feels like hitting something—he grips a cardboard coaster in one hand and snaps it in two. His mind starts to wander… He remembers being a kid and being scared of dogs. Everyone used to tell him to stop being so scared—to just fight through it. And finally he listened. And he tried to pet that German Shepherd. And guess what happened? That dog bit the shit out of his hand. Fuck dogs. Fuck all those people.

He drinks a whole pitcher of Pabst and orders another.

At least he came to the right place—it's a country dive bar, but pitchers are only five dollars on Thursdays. As he starts in on number two, a girl in a wool sweater sits on the stool next to him and orders a Long Island. He tells her that that drink has gotten him in trouble before, and considers telling her about getting punched in the nose by the blond chick, but decides to bite his tongue. She seems cool and talks to him, telling him that she's here from out of town and came with her mom and brother, who are on their way. *Great.*

It's easy to talk to her because he's a little bit drunk and she's not overly attractive. She tells him about her aunt's wedding this weekend and he talks about how he always has fun at weddings. Then her mom walks in with her brother and Nick can't believe the woman is her mom—sexy outfit, hair, make-up—even though she's with her kids and in her late forties, she looks like she's out to score. The daughter is kind of cute, but not sexy like the mom, and definitely dressed like her priority is to stay warm.

"I went to one wedding in college—we drank so much they turned the bar into a cash bar," Nick says.

"Yeah, I don't think this one will be like that," she says. "Probably just a bunch of old people getting wasted."

"Excuse me?!" her mom says, laughing, and then whispers something in her daughter's ear.

"My mom thinks you're cute—she likes to point out guys for me even though I have a boyfriend."

"Right on," Nick says. "Yeah, I'm trying to enjoy the single life, but it's harder than you think. See, you females, you guys have it easy."

"I can't stand when guys call us *females*," she interrupts. "like we're some kind of foreign species!"

"You're not a foreign species?" he asks. "What are we supposed to say?"

"Women, or I think even girls is better than *females*," she says, giggling and sipping her drink.

"Can I please get back to my story?" Nick asks as he leans in and bumps his knee into her leg. "You *women* have it easy. All you have to do is go to a bar, have a drink, and guys come up to you. Us, we have to go out there and try to start up a conversation. It's a lot of work."

"Poor you—I can tell you have a lot of trouble doing that," she says. "And you're working *really* hard right now." She pets his arm to make him feel better.

"See, that's because you have a boyfriend. I knew it was too good to be true—a sexy female—lady—coming up and sitting by me. And then on top of that, she's cool?"

"Well if I wasn't in a relationship, I would be interested," she says, and nudges him with her elbow.

Nick keeps drinking and he can see her beauty more and more clearly with each beer. She orders another Long Island.

"Here's the problem with relationships," Nick says, "when the person starts holding you down. In my next relationship, I'm just gonna let the girl do whatever she wants, and I'm gonna just be there for her. And she can support me. That's all I'm doing. Whatever she wants to do, I'll let her do it, and I'll help her so she can do it. Like, there doesn't have to be any holding each other back. That's what I hate about relationships—it should be all positive."

"I know. That's how my relationship started out, and now it's mostly like that, but sometimes it feels like it's starting to change, like he's trying to make sure he knows where I am all the time and everything. But he's good to me." Nick looks over at the brother and the mom, and he's glad the brother doesn't care that he's talking to his sister. Nick finishes the second pitcher, takes a piss, and then thinks about ordering another pitcher but decides to just get a pint.

"So what are you guys gonna do tonight?" he asks, leaning into her and softly nudging the side of her butt with his hand.

"I think we're going back to the hotel," she says.

"Let me drive you back to the hotel," Nick says, dick on pole.

"I don't know." She turns to her mom and then turns back to him. "Are you sure you want to give us a ride back there?"

"I want to give *you* a ride back there so we can hang out for a minute," he says.

"I can't. I can't do that to my boyfriend."

"I just want to hang out with you for a minute," he says in her ear, feeling on her stomach. She lets him. He turns to her mom. "You think it's that big a deal if I give her a ride back to the hotel and you guys meet her a little later?"

The mom smiles at her daughter and Nick. She likes him. "It's not like you're married," she says to her daughter.

"Thank you!" Nick says. "You're not married. You can always work stuff out with your little boyfriend." Then he leans in again and whispers. "I really wanna break you off." Now he's talking like Marcus from the sign shop—he said that the other day.

"I'm sorry, I wish I could, but he would never do that to me. But let me have your number, okay? If stuff doesn't work out, I'll give you a call." Then she leans into him, "and I'll break *you* off."

Nick gives her his number and leaves the bar. Damn he wanted to fuck her. There's something about a girl that wants you so much she'll almost cheat on her man.

He's looking for a girl to talk to, but Alex in the hospital bed pops back in his head. That face… his broken nose held into place, stitches across his cheek bone, bruises around his eyes and one eye that looked like the eyeball itself was bleeding. He shakes it off. Who could he call right now?

He tries the girl from a couple weeks ago, who never called him back, and of course she doesn't pick up. Fuck, maybe he should have tried to hook up with the mom at the bar. No, the daughter was cool, and that would've been fucked up.

He passes his car and decides he's too drunk to drive, and plus, he's not ready for sleep yet—he knows if he tried going to sleep now he would just be lying there thinking about Alex, picturing that near-death facial expression. So he starts walking down Patriot Blvd, past the Subway and the Wachovia. A black kid who's about Nick's size, and a few years younger, is walking up the other side of the street. Nick watches him looking all around himself, and wonders if he's on the run from somewhere. The kid looks paranoid. Then he starts walking fast across the street to Nick. "What's up, bro?" Nick says.

"Ain't no what's up, give me your fucking money and your wallet!" The boy is grabbing in his pants like he's going to pull out a gun, and then holds his shirt out like he's covering up a pistol.

"You have a gun in there?" Nick says.

"Break yourself," the kid says.

"If you show me your gun, I'll give you ten dollars. If you don't, then get the fuck out of my face." It's so obvious the boy doesn't have a gun, just from the vibe of him. And why would you do the fake gun thing if there's no one around? But just in case, Nick stands close so that if he's wrong, he'll be able to punch him in the face before he draws it out. "I think there's an elementary school up the block," Nick says. "You can wait for school to start and try that with them." Nick is too faded to be scared of something like that.

"You lucky I'ma let you live today, whiteboy," the kid says as he back pedals away, trying to look hard.

"Right," Nick says, and keeps walking. He's full of energy all of a sudden and regrets not swinging at the kid. Maybe that would have erased Alex's bloody face from his mind. Fuck, he can't stop thinking about it. If he would have gone home with the chick he would have been okay—damn he wanted to fuck.

He goes into a bar to check out the females and use the bathroom. There are a few dudes and no females, so he heads to the bathroom and takes a piss in the urinal. He clears his throat, leans forward, and spits onto the deodorizer puck.

"That's disgusting," someone says from the sink.

"Spitting in the bathroom is disgusting?" Nick says without looking up.

"For someone as cute as you, it is," he says. Nick looks over and sees a well-dressed guy a few years older than he is, looking at him suggestively. "And I never spit," he says, his eyes moving down Nick's body.

"Bro." Nick shakes his head. "*That's* disgusting," he says, still peeing.

"Is it though? You don't like it when people swallow?"

He doesn't know what to say. There are mirrors all around the bathroom and he sees the man's line of vision ricocheting straight to his dick. There's no point in cussing him out—the guy is harmless—he's just hitting on him. Like, hard. Nick keeps peeing. Is this guy serious? Does he really just want Nick's dick, without even knowing him? That's something he's only seen in pornos, because girls for some reason never just come out and hit on dudes like that—like just basically tell them they want some dick.

Nick keeps peeing, but his dick begins to firm up, and he wants to stop it because the guy is still standing there, so he blocks it with his hand and points it downward. He can feel the man watching him, and focuses his own eyes down at the clear stream as it slows through his erection.

"I live a half a block away—come by for a nightcap," the guy says, and jots an address down on the back of a business card and then slides it into Nick's back pocket. Nick fumbles his erection back into his jeans. He feels the man's hand slide up from his jeans, the flesh of fingers ducking under his shirt and onto his skin, pressing into his stomach briefly and then pulling, slightly rocking him back into the man's body before Nick moves to the side, his breath rising.

"Bro," Nick says.

"I'll leave the door unlocked," he whispers, and leaves.

Nick washes his face and dries it with a paper towel. He tries to finish peeing but it's no use—his dick is rock hard. He goes outside, bums a cigarette, and looks at the address—1402 Lenox. The next block on his way home is Lenox. *Fuck.*

He's got to at least check it out, so he walks up the row of townhouses until he gets to 1402. His entire body comes alive and he tries to shake it out of him as he turns the knob and the door grants him access. "You came fast!" says the man from what must be the kitchen. "I'm finishing up the drinks—come down to my room."

"Right on," Nick says under his breath. The space is open, broken up only by furniture. He walks through the living room area and into the bedroom and stands there. There's a skylight that looks dark and opaque above the bed.

"I made us Manhattans," the man says. Nick thanks him and they clink glasses. "You're even cuter than you were ten minutes ago. What's your name?"

First he thinks of Frank, but that sounds too made-up, then he thinks of Pablo, but that sounds too Latino. "Josh," he says.

"You're lying—I'm Joshua," the guy says. Nick realizes that he saw the guy's name on the business card and wonders if that's why he said it.

"You thought you were the only one named that?" Nick says. He sips his cocktail.

"No," Joshua says. "I just didn't know we had so much in com-mon." He touches Nick's neck and then pets him down his chest to his stomach to the crotch of his jeans. "Have you ever been with a man before?"

Nick drinks his drink. "No—I don't do that kind of thing."

"Let me show you the ropes." He takes Nick's hand and guides it onto the front of his own slacks. Nick leaves his hand limp but does not pull back—and the hard indentation on the man's slacks gives him an intense shock. He flashes back to when he was twelve and he stole a pack of Fun Dip for the first time and no one found out. No one was in the area, but the laws of the land were watching and seemed to be talking to him. *Thou shalt not steal. Thou shalt not touch another man's dick.*

He looks up at the skylight and pulls his hand back, the dark night sky peeking down on him. What's up there? Who's behind that glass? He should go. No, he should stay—why not? It's okay to do something...

"You wanna, like, suck my dick?" Nick says.

"Woah, woah, woah. Slow down—I'm not a ho," Joshua says, shaking his finger at Nick. "You think you're just going to come in here, pull it out, and have me drop to my knees and start sucking you off?" He presses his palm flat against Nick's crotch and moves it in slow circles. Nick tries not to breathe loud. "Is that what you think?" He unbuckles Nick's belt and then slides his zipper down. Nick doesn't say anything. Joshua drags the pants all the way down. And then, from his knees: "So you think you're just gonna stand there and I'm just gonna take care of this beautiful dick? Is that what you think?" Joshua massages Nick's erection through his boxers, and then pinches the fabric on both sides and slowly lowers the underpants until his dick springs free. "Is that what you think?" He teases the tip with his tongue, and Nick wants to grab the back of Joshua's head, but resists—that might be gay.

Nick watches as the man alternates between tongue play and taking him into his mouth. It's weird seeing a man down there, but damn it feels good. The guy is just so into it.

He hears a helicopter in the distance, and looks up at the sky-light. Are they spying on him? There must be surveillance. Maybe Joshua works for the FBI? He must have hidden cameras set up. Or maybe it's God that he's sensing. Who is it? "I shouldn't be doing this," Nick says.

"I know—you're a bad boy," Joshua says. And then he takes Nick's hand and places it on the back of his head. "Give it to me," he says, like a girl would, and closes his eyes. Nick's penis pumps even bigger and he thrusts a few times into Joshua's mouth before exploding. "Yessss," the guy says.

That's fucking nasty.

Joshua's on his knees with the hint of a smile tilted up—he rubs Nick's leg all the way up to the ass and back down. It's hard to tell what the dude wants. Is there a certain protocol for these sorts of things? Nick pulls his pants back on. "I would love to like, return the favor, or whatever, but I have to be at work at seven in the morning," Nick says.

"I don't want you to return the favor. I knew exactly what I was getting myself into—and I got exactly what I wanted," he says. "Now zip up your fly before you leave so your girlfriend doesn't know you went to a gay bar."

"Gay bar?"

Joshua laughs.

"Really?" Nick smiles. "Wow." He shakes his head.

As he walks along the sidewalk, he feels sober. He thinks about the girl and her mom and her brother and the boy without a gun and Joshua. Joshua—he got head from a man… But Joshua just walked up and offered it, that's why. That's basically what happened. It's not like Nick dropped to his knees and started going at the guy. It's not like he did that. Even though he could have. He saw his dick pressing hard against the black fabric of his pants. But he didn't make a move for it—didn't release it and start going at it, seeing if he could give the guy the same satisfaction that he got. He definitely didn't do that.

And he rotates these things around in his head, because whenever Alex and his frightened and doomed expression pop back in his head, he can distract the thought with the other shit that happened tonight.

When he gets to his apartment, he puts some Oriental Raman noodles in a bowl with some water and then puts them in the microwave for three minutes. He sees a leftover roach sitting on the table, so he picks it up, lights it, and takes a drag. It doesn't pull, so he raises it up to his low eyelids. Fuck, it isn't a blunt roach at all—it's a real fucking roach. A dead roach… huh. No wonder they call them that. He drops it on the floor and lies down on the couch until his noodles are ready. His lids fall over and he's out cold by the time the microwave beeps.

Chapter 20 — Ramona

"Drama, get down! Get off of there!" Ramona hears Quint yelling at the dog and wakes up. She hears licking. Her body feels like it weighs a thousand pounds, hot and heavy on the mattress.

"Drama get down! Get off!" There's yelling and there're dogs licking and all she wants to do is fall back into sleep. But she can't. Someone's shaking her. It's Quint.

"What? What?" she says, and then stuffs her head into the pillow.

"It's blood all over you!" he says. Flashes of Quint's face are replaced with flashes of thick dark red blotches on sheets and light patches of strawberries on her stomach. She flips onto her hands and knees and then off the bed, surveying the blood stained linens.

"Shit," she says, the reality of what's happened hitting her. He's going to be pissed off. The first time she sleeps over and this happens? Fuck!

"Are you okay? What happened? I just woke up and Drama was licking on the blood."

"I'm so sorry. I didn't think it was coming for like three days," she says.

"What wasn't coming for like three days?" Quint says, and then, "Oh. Fuck." He realizes, takes a deep breath and then slowly exhales and his head gyrates along with his deflating chest. "Thank god. That wasn't cool. I mean, not what you did. I just didn't know it was period and everything. My brain was going in a whole different direction."

"I don't know what to say," Ramona says.

"Drama, get back! Get your ass away from there!" Quint yells, and scoops up a pillow and chest passes it at the dog, who's found a bloody corner of the blanket and is licking it. He misses. The dog looks up apologetically with her eyes, but at the same time her tongue continues gathering the flavor of period.

Ramona's head floats in and out of reality. She sees him throwing things and she sees blood and dogs. He must be angry. How is she going to get out of this situation? What if he really flips out? What has she gotten herself into? She closes her eyes for a second and is back at that place—drifts back two years ago. At the warehouse. Partying.

Drinks. Lines of powder on backs of toilets. Everything. And then she was walking home and she was walking home with Lowell. He had been cool. There was no problem with him. He said he wanted to walk her home. They had been teasing each other and so she said she knows how to walk—her mom taught her how when she was one. He said he insists—he's going to take her home. And they walked, and it was fine. It was fine. And then he wanted to kiss. She didn't want to kiss—she wanted to sleep. She was hitting a wall and wanted to sleep. He followed her in when she undid the lock. She said thanks and everything and said she just needs to go to sleep. He kept following her. She said she had to go to the bathroom and so he should go. And then he reached for her. His coward fake smile left his face and everything changed.

If only she could have shot him in the head the way he was on top of her. But she had to just be there, beneath him. And she couldn't understand where God was. God needed to stop this from happening. He was supposed to come in with laser beams and explode the rapist into nothing. But he didn't. When Lowell was pinning her down and open, she erupted with all the noise she could, but he blocked it with his hand and then he blocked it with the pillow.

So she left that place.

And she tries not to hold it against good men.

She tries.

"It ain't you," Quint says. "I don't have no problem with a period. You could have your period around my whole room far as I could care." He picks up the clean side of the blanket. "Let's see. Let's get these out of here." He bunches them up. "And drink this water."

She drinks. Her eyes change from fear to affection. She can't help it.

Bloody pajamas and covers and all, she climbs over to him and presses her chest into him. It's like she can feel his pulse through everything. She looks down and sees what she is doing. "Okay, I'm seriously deranged, giving you a bloody hug." They lean on each other and laugh. "Where's your washer and dryer—I'll put these in," she adds.

"Don't worry about it, I'll take care of it," Quint says, and kisses her on the forehead.

"No, seriously, let me do this."

"We don't even do laundry, like, in the house. We go out to do it."

"Oh, right. Like a laundromat. Yeah yeah yeah. Totally," she says. Fuck, why'd she say that? That probably sounded so judgmental. "I mean, can I like…" He's got to have cleaning supplies, right? "get something to clean the mattress with, and then I'll take the laundry."

"It's all good—I got it."

"Quintavious," she says, lowering her eyes, her hand on the doorknob. "Where are your cleaning supplies?"

"Don't try to sound like my mama," he smiles. "They under the sink. It should be a garbage bag under there too. Can you please change out of them bloody clothes though? I can't have no," he hesitates. What was he going to say, white girl? Bloody white girl? "I can't have you walking around the house looking like you got sprayed in a drive-by."

He gives her some sweatpants and she marches into the kitchen, wishing Marcus *would* be there. She finds some Oxy Clean and a garbage bag. They move the mattress onto the balcony and Ramona wants to do it herself but Quint insists on helping her. They scrub the blood, fall into each other cracking up, and then Ramona packs up the laundry and leaves.

Chapter 21 – Marcus

Marcus's eyes shudder under their lids. The corner of his mouth twitches towards his ear. His body lies stomach down on the asphalt underneath the parked squad car—his head barely able to look up without bumping the engine. Old florescent lights buzz and struggle to stay on, trying to keep the shadows from creeping into the parking lot.

Marcus's fingers wrap around the cold steel of the .45, heavy in his hand—his trigger finger itching to lighten the load. He is there for one reason—to right a wrong. To bring justice. He must lay that motherfucker down to rest. Put that rabid dog out of his misery. God rest his soul, the son of a bitch, or let him burn in hell for killing Dad.

The elevator door opens into the parking lot and out comes the cop. Step by step towards the cruiser. He knows not what he does. Closer he comes, cupping his hands together—breathing into them—it's a cold night for a homicide.

Purple lips—Mountain Dew—chasing after Quint—electrocuting Quint off the back gate—blasting bullet holes through Dad—cop walks closer. Steam comes out of his nose—*unsafe, unscared, nigga*—Psycho—step, step—*do it now!*—tilting his aim to the middle of the cop chest—step, step—*it's time to squeeze—it's time to squeeze!*—his finger paralyzed—*why won't it move?— squeeze!*—*he's a motherfucking murderer!*—dry purple lips—step, step—three feet away—*squeeze!*—cop reaches into his jacket—an enormous set of keys fall to the pavement and settle in six inches away from Marcus's face. Point blank—he'll be lined up perfect. Down he squats, scooping the keys—holding them in front of Marcus like a ripped out heart. His cop eyes staring. He knows what happened, but his face is calm—a trace of a smile that won't go away—*squeeze!*—cop eyes stay staring—challenging—*squeeze!—do it now*!

But nothing. Marcus watches his own body stay still, not following the orders from his mind—his finger not budging. His arm not moving. The cop is the only thing moving—his crusty cop hand reaching up towards Marcus's gun, and slowly taking hold of the barrel—*now is the time!—squeeze!*—nothing—frozen still—the cop grips and controls the gun—he rotates it—Marcus's powerless hand controlled by the cop's—the murderer reaches with his other hand—big and pink and dry—and presses it into Marcus's neck—digs his cop finger in the side of Marcus's throat and guides Marcus's head scraping into the concrete. *Kill this man! End this man!* The cracks of purple and pink leak blood as the cop smiles—

strength!—*move!*—now only Marcus's head can move—it begins to shake—whipping around—*escape!*— *kill!*—*escape!*—*move!*

Marcus wakes up, shaking, breathing out of his mouth, and searches the ceiling for answers. Why does he keep having this dream? Why can he never pull the trigger?

Chapter 22 – Ramona

Ramona holds the pile of linens in front of her as she walks up to Q's door and hits *07. The buzzer doesn't work so she has to wait for somebody to come down. It's times like these when her "no phone, just stop by" policy isn't very effective—she's still cramping and she just feels like shit. Her breath hits the air and turns to steam and she waits, in her sweater, scarf and backpack, thinking about who would be more awkward to see right now, his mom, because they've never met, or Marcus… Why didn't she just bring a tote bag to leave in a hiding place for Quint to pick up? She hears steps and then Marcus swings open the door and stands wide in the doorway like he's guarding his property—one of those wife beater tank tops, she hates that term, with an unzipped black jacket, the one Quint was wearing with the fake fur around the hood, some sweatpants, and some slippers.

"Uhh!" Ramona says in relief. "Thank god you're home. These are Quint's sheets." She balances herself with a mound of linens in her arms and a textbook-filled backpack on her shoulders.

"Them are my sheets," Marcus says. Even though he's only a small step up from her, he looks down at her like he's on a balcony. "Why are you here?"

"To return Quint's linens." *Duh?*

"He ain't here," Marcus says.

"Well I sorta wanted to go in and put them on his bed, as like a gesture and everything." He probably doesn't know about the period, and that's probably for the better.

"I can't let you in the house without Quint being here," Marcus says in a relaxed way—like he enjoys the small power, the small authority, that he has.

A strong cramp hits Ramona and she suddenly loses all patience. "What are you, ten years old?"

Marcus smiles, apparently enjoying the challenge. "I was raised to where if white people in sheets show up at your door, you don't let them in."

He did *not* just make that reference. "Just take the fucking sheets."

"Don't get a attitude with me—this is my security system—we ain't got no ONSTAR like y'all got. I gotta watch out for agent provocateurs."

Yeah I'm a fucking agent provocateur doing laundry for Quint so I can infiltrate your apartment and find some pot. "Can you take the sheets so I can go?"

"Just put them down."

Jesus Christ. "I'm not gonna put them down in the mud."

Marcus yawns. "Quint gets back at seven, you could come back then."

In one motion, Ramona launches the neat pile six feet through the air, into Marcus's chin like a bank shot, and then plop, into his instinctively outstretched arms.

She stomps away, and then turns back—Marcus is holding the sheets against his chest, with his chin peaking over and exposing an ear-to-ear smile.

She smiles back at him and shakes her head. "You fucking asshole," she jokes, and heads home.

Chapter 23 – Nick

"So you don't eat no meat? No chicken, no beef, no pork?" Marcus says, the letters on his tattoos now looking puffy and dark.

Nick is walking back from his lunch break with a cheese and veggie sandwich. He hasn't really said anything the whole day at work, and doesn't really feel like talking, but answers the question anyway. "No."

"What about fish, that ain't meat?"

"Bro—what else would it be, a plant? And why would I kill an animal just to eat it? Would you go up to a little dog and just kill it and put it in the microwave?" Nick's only been a vegetarian for two months but right now he feels like defending his point. Luana comes in the back and is writing notes on a work order before putting it on the wall. It's impossible not to hear her heels and smell her perfume whenever she's near.

"I don't eat dog," Marcus says.

"But you eat other animals. There's no difference," Nick says.

"I don't kill nothing, I just buy that mug from Save-a-lot, take it to the house, and cook it up, you feel me?"

Nick lets a big breath fall from his nose like it's painful for him to explain this. And even though he knows Luana is listening and would normally freeze up in front of her, today he doesn't give a fuck. He hasn't given a fuck since Alex got jumped. "The reason they kill it is so people like you can eat it. If you're too scared to kill it, you shouldn't be able to eat it. It's like hiring a hit man to kill your enemy, bro. At least the people hunting know what the animal went through to get on their plate." Nick pauses for a second. "I'm not gonna murder to have a good taste in my mouth."

"A nigga can't live on collard greens and tomatoes." He looks at Julio, "and god damn bean burritos. Fuck that."

Nick sees Luana still bent over the work order, scribbling a million words per minute. "Have you ever noticed how pretty mixed babies are? Like, especially when they're white and black and Filipino?" Nick says.

"This fool…" Julio shakes his head.

Luana looks up. "I'm already mixed so my babies will turn out mixed no matter what."

"Oh, what's up Luana? I didn't even see you there—I was talking to my production team," Nick says.

"Aaaaaah, she was thinking about it!" Charles says.

Before she can respond with a comeback, Gary storms into the back, holding one of Marcus's signs. "Who the hell made this?"

"That was mine," Marcus says.

"And you sent it out like this?" Gary says. Marcus doesn't say anything. "Is this a good sign to you?" Marcus doesn't say anything. "Hey, boy, I'm talking to you. Is this a good sign?"

"No," Marcus says.

"What's wrong with this sign?"

"The letters is a little bit crooked."

"The letters is a little bit crooked? And why *is* the letters a little bit crooked—did you not use the fucking crop marks to line it up?"

"I don't think that one had crop marks on it."

"All the fucking signs have crop marks on them, son. You probably forgot to leave the fucking marks on when you weeded it. Okay? And not only that, but all of you, don't ever send out a sign like this to a customer. You got that?" No response. "Huh! Anybody here? I'm not talking to myself. I'll hire a whole new production crew today if you want. Do, you, understand, what, I'm, talking, about? Respond to the fucking question."

"Yes," says Marcus.

"Yes sir," says Julio.

"Yeah," says Nick. Gary goes out the front, giving them some peace.

"See, he a racist ass cracker. No offense Nick," Marcus says.

"No, he not racist," Charles says. "You shoulda seen him chew Nick a new asshole the second day he was here. He don't discriminate—he treats everybody like shit. You never know what day could be your last. I've known Gary for seven years. He fired me twice. He don't care. If you fuck up on the wrong day, you gone," Charles says.

"But I'm saying, my nigga, if that woulda been me on Friday? Like Nick, not coming to work. Not calling. Fuck that, I'da been fired."

Nick responds in a quiet, serious voice. "My brother got jumped Thursday night. Had to go to the hospital."

"For real?" Charles says. "I thought he didn't leave the house? This your brother that's sick in the head, right?"

"Yeah. He finally got a job and was delivering pizza over at the University and then got jumped."

"Damn," Charles says, shaking his head. "That ain't right. This man finally makes it out the house and gets him a job—and I know your mama was happy about that—and then he gets his ass jumped. Mmmm. Ain't no justice."

"He'll be back in his room now—with my mom taking care of him," Nick says.

Marcus works on his sign with his head down.

The production room stays quiet until it finally becomes six o'clock and they can clock out. Nick is driving out of the parking lot when he sees Luana walking to the train station. "Need a ride?" he says.

She steps in his direction.

"Hop in. Sorry about the mess—I let my brother borrow it the other day and this is how I get it back." Nick grabs an empty Power Aid bottle, a few cd cases and an old box of Cheeze-Its and throws them in the back of his pick-up. He's been meaning to clean this shit for a while, and feels a little bit guilty for blaming it on Alex, but, that's what brothers are for.

"So, was your day better than mine?" she says, with perfect body posture. Most of the time, Luana speaks like she does when she's talking to customers—very polite and enunciating every part of every word.

"Mine was okay," Nick says. "Why was yours so bad? Gary getting on your nerves?"

"No, I know how to deal with Gary. It's that Phillip and I aren't getting along and I don't know what to do."

Phillip is her boyfriend. He knows from his coworkers that he's a white guy—but why is she choosing to talk about him right now? Fuck, his gas is below empty. "Um, I guess you should drop him if you guys aren't getting along." What else is he supposed to say?

"I just feel so bad. He's a really good friend and I've known him since middle school." She's completely different outside of work. Her defenses come down and he can actually talk to her.

"You should do what you want to do." Nick drives past Taco Bell and wants to get a couple burritos, but decides to wait until he drops off Luana. A seven layer burrito would be nice…

They drive without talking for a few blocks—the clutch grinding and the stick shift jerking about like it's arm wrestling with Nick. Luana flips down the tiny mirror on the top side of the visor and examines her face.

"So you live in the Community, right?" he says. It's a small area of houses, cottages, and apartments right near the bars and cafés on the east side where a lot of young hipsters and artist-type people live. It used to be cool but now it's expensive and kind of commercial and bourgie.

"Yes, just take a right up here," Luana says as her phone rings. She picks up, "Hi hun, I already got a ride… Nick… He just got hired the other day in Production… No don't worry about it… Can you drive me to my mom's later on though, at around eight?… Okay, I have to go… Bye… Yeah I love you too… Bye." What a herb…

They pass some graffiti and Nick stares, recognizes it as his brother's style. Luana sees him looking and then reads it, "2 beers a diaper and some tin foil," then does a fake laugh. "Sounds like a *memoire*," she says, and does it with the French accent and everything. "I drank two beers and the next thing I knew I was changing diapers and smoking crack out of some tin foil."

"You're fucking weird," Nick says without thinking, and they both laugh.

"There's no one in the driveway so why don't you park there and come in for a drink," Luana says.

He really probably shouldn't, but can't help himself and follows her up the steps, her perfect booty, long thick hair, and smooth skin impossible to ignore. Her little apartment looks like a hotel room—everything is clean and all the colors are whites and light grays. She even has a gray cat that seems to match. "That's Bella the princess—she'll whoop your ass," Luana says with a laugh—sounding like Beavis and Butthead.

"Hey Bella," Nick says, but doesn't touch her.

"I'm sorry, all I've got is Bacardi, Smirnoff, and I also have some *Merlot*." She does it again—the accent thing. "And to mix we have a choice of Coke, Fruit punch, or there's always my favorite, on the rocks."

Ok, well . "Rum and Coke please." She brings the drinks back and takes a seat across from Nick and has a smile on her face like she's trying to do well in an interview for a job. The funny thing is that Nick knows she grew up on the west side in the 130s, deep in the hood. "Why do you act so proper if you grew up in the hood?" he asks.

"Why do you try to act ghetto if you grew up on 65th street?" she says back to him. How does she know where he grew up?

"I don't act ghetto. I act the same way I always acted. You think all white people are squares?"

"No, but just because I grew up in the hood, doesn't mean I got raised to be ghetto. I've been smart and motivated my whole life, and if me knowing I'm going to be someone and not letting where I was born determine how I act makes me a square, then you can think what you want," she counters.

"I was just wondering," Nick says with a smile. She blushes and walks into the kitchen. He loves that quick tongue—she just broke it down.

"So why did you drop out of the university?" Luana asks.

"I didn't," Nick says. He stands up and walks along the blank wall, drinking his drink. "They kicked me out." He crunches a piece of ice, "for being a vegetarian."

"Whatever. You dropped out."

"They kicked me out. I'm serious!" he says. "I gave a speech in class on vegetarianism, right? And they couldn't handle the truth so they kicked me out. I swear." He pretends he's focusing really hard on a single flower sticking out of a vase. "I had to give a persuasive speech in public speaking class, right? So I chose vegetarianism. My whole point is that people don't know what they're eating. They don't see a pepperoni as a dead pig—they don't see lamb as a dead baby sheep getting murdered. So my job is to persuade them to recognize the process so they make the moral decision to stop eating meat, right?"

"You dropped out."

"So the day before my speech, I happen to catch a mouse in my five gallon bucket trap. It's a live trap." Luana sits on the couch, watching Nick pace back and forth and start gesturing with his hands. "You take a five gallon bucket, right? You set up a ramp leading up to the rim. You tie a piece of fishing line across the top of the bucket. In the middle of the line, you put an aluminum can with some peanut butter on it. Mouse walks up the ramp, jumps onto the can to get the peanut butter, can spins on the fishing line, down goes the mouse, into the bucket."

"I kill mice," Luana says.

"So at the end of my speech, I take out an empty glass fish tank with the mouse inside. I put on a white glove, take the lid off, and smash the mouse until it dies."

"Awesome," she says.

"Exactly. A demonstration. Just so they know that animals are actually getting killed to give them that meat. And guess what?" Nick opens his eyes wide and darts his head side to side. "They freaked out! Yeah! They would rather stay blind to the process, and when I come along to shed light, they kick me out."

"You better not be lying."

"Why would I lie about something like that?" Nick says with a high pitch and a grin.

Luana looks him down. "Another drink?"

"I gotta go. I'll take a road soda if you got it." He doesn't want to act like he's trying to steal her from her man, but he is thinking it would be nice if she left him. She mixes him a drink in a plastic cup and he takes it. He gets his keys and offers an awkward hand-shake as he heads out the door.

"I don't shake hands with guys," she says, and hugs him.

Chapter 24 – Quintavious

Quint still wouldn't move. He was supposed to be at work twenty minutes ago, but couldn't budge from his bed. "Bruh! Get up! You can't keep doing this!" Marcus says. There's no response. "They're finna fire you, bruh." Marcus has been trying to act all responsible ever since he got a job.

"It's whatever," Quint says.

"Ain't no whatever, bruh, you gotta get that paper."

"Fuck paper," he groans, curled around his covers away from Marcus.

"We got bills, bruh. Even my ass is workin."

"Bills, pocket money, food… That's what I'm working for? That's my future? That's my life? I'm good, bruh. Y'all can do all that."

"That ain't your future, bruh. It's how you see it." Marcus steps up closer to the bed. "It's 2009, nigga, ain't no limits except what you put on yourself. I swear to God, bruh, you could live on a island surfing thirty foot waves if you really wanted to."

Quint just lies there.

"We got control over our…" Marcus starts.

"Get off that pipe, nigga. Ain't no surfers in the hood," Quint says. "What am I really gonna do? I ain't no smart motherfucker. I ain't gonna be no doctor or lawyer or athlete or rapper. That's what they forget about. If you that one smartest motherfucker in the class, then you could make it out. If you ain't, then shit… you ain't shit, then."

Quint rolls from his stomach to his side, propping his head up with his elbow. He looks dead at Marcus. "Think about this, bruh. White people try to work in the hood, right? Teachers and shit. What happens to most of them?"

"They try but they can't fuck with us, so they leave after a couple years."

"Exactly, bruh. So they can't fuck with our community, so they go back to they community. Then what happens?"

"I don't know, bruh, it depend."

"Exactly, bruh. They got a million jobs in they community, making *money*. They ain't gotta work in our community. They ain't gotta relate to our community. They ain't gotta have shit to do with our community."

"And?"

"And then look at us, bruh. We try to work in they community, and it's the same shit as them. Some of us can do it and it's all good. But just like them, most of us can't fuck with their community like that. So what happens to us? What do we got to fall back on? We ain't got shit, bruh. Manual labor, nigga, making they shit better. Security, nigga, guarding they shit."

"So you making the black business argument—that we should own our own shit?"

"Nigga I'm making my own argument—don't paint me in a box, nigga."

"I'm just sayin, bruh, you can't play the victim and make excuses—that's what they want you to do."

"Okay, bruh, you stay on that pipe then. You can be whateeeeeever you want in life. You could be president. Why don't you do me a favor and go try for president, bruh, and let me know how that works out for you." Quint rolls back onto his stomach.

"Why don't you stay in bed all day every day and let me know how that works for you, nigga." Marcus walks out.

Chapter 25 – Marcus

"You broke already?" asks Big Lenny as they walk through Thousand Oaks Park.

"Nigga you seen my tattoos—that shit ain't free," Marcus says. "And you know how fast money go—if you don't spend it on something you actually want, it'll be gone on some bullshit and you not gonna have shit to show for it, you feel me?"

"Whatever, bruh. Just make sure you hold dub for next week 'cause the session on you."

"I got you man. It's good. The fuck your goofy-ass all stressed out for?"

"I'm trying to get some p-p-pussy my nigga."

"I hear that. Matter of fact, me too," Marcus says. "Let me hold your phone one time."

"Who you calling?"

"Lasandra," Marcus dials the number. "Yeah you know who this is, right? Yeah, what's happening? Where you been? Not shit, I been around. I been looking for you. Naw, you called? My mama ain't told me nothing. Shit, you don't have to say it like that, I thought *you* wasn't trying to talk to *me*? Alright, call me back on Lenny phone." Marcus hangs up and looks at Lenny. "Damn, why hoes be trippin when you don't talk to them for a minute. It's like if you hit it, you gotta keep hittin that shit or else you *not* gonna be able to hit it."

"Like a joint, nigga. You ever notice how you gotta keep hittin a joint else it'll go out on you?"

"Yeah. Thank you! Females is like a muthafuckin joint. Niggas is like a blunt—you could hit us once, let a nigga chill for a while, then come back and you still be able to hit us again!"

"Hell yeah. But hey, look who that is up on the corner—Tasha. She's a god damn blunt right there. At least for yo ass, bruh."

"That's what I was about to say—she a god damn blunt. Straight up!" Marcus says, falling into Lenny with laughter.

"Ta-sha!" Marcus says to her. She smiles and says hi. "Look at that smile. Girl, you got a million dollar smile." She blushes and says thank you, trying to look cute. "I bet you wish you had a trillion dollar smile like me though."

"Nigga shut your skinny-ass up. It's like, here come slim and fat. Slim fat. Not slim fast, slim fat."

"Yeah ha ha we get it," says Lenny.

Tasha is still laughing at her own joke, "That's what I'm finna call y'all from now on, Slim Fat."

"I'ma call you blunt," Lenny says.

"Blunt?" she says.

"Don't worry about it." Marcus and Lenny say at the same time.

"But on the real though, Tasha, I been trying to talk to you about rapping," Marcus says. "You gonna come with us to the studio? We need a female for a couple tracks."

"Hell yeah, nigga, you know that. But I don't know if y'all could afford me though."

"How much you charge, two Reese cups and a Snicker?"

"That'll work," she says, and they all start laughing. "When y'all going?"

"Right now. Let's go."

"That's what's up." The three of them continue walking up Patriot Blvd.

"I need to get my rhymes from the crib—I got some serious fire this week, boi!" Lenny says.

"I gotta get my shit, too," Marcus says. "I'ma go with Tasha and we'll meet you at the station."

"If you ain't there I'm leaving, my nigga," Lenny says. "The music industry ain't no joke, it's a business, I don't have time to be…"

"Shut your lame ass up, nigga, we'll be there."

"Alright," Lenny says, smiling. "Ay don't hit that blunt without me," he chuckles.

They start down the block, and Marcus runs his hand down Tasha's hair, pressing lightly on her neck, trying to see if she's in the mood. "I thought Lenny don't even smoke?" she says.

"He don't—he just talking about some different shit, don't worry about it," Marcus says as they walk over to his apartment and go in his room. Marcus and Tasha have hooked up a couple times, and he likes her—she's fun to hang out with, she's funny, and she's a freak in bed. She looks cool too. The main reason she doesn't get more respect is because she's been with so many guys.

"So you ready to hit the studio or you wanna chill here for a minute?"

"I'm ready to lay them tracks down," she says. Marcus thinks about saying that he's ready to lay that pipe down, but bites his tongue.

"You seem like you a little stressed out though. You know it's not good to sing when you stressed." Marcus starts massaging her shoulders.

"First of all, nigga, we rappin, you s'posed to be stressed out, you ain't s'posed to be relaxed and calm when you rappin. Second of all, what happened to your game? I thought you had a little bit of game at least." She's trying to say no but Marcus knows she likes him. In fact, she likes him more than he likes her.

"I don't play games, girl, I'm just real. I'm just me. I guess you right, you don't need no massage to rap," he says, and stops rubbing her neck. He gives her a look like *it's your decision.*

"How much time we got anyway?"

"Not long," Marcus says and walks in front of her, putting on his pretty face. He can tell by the look in her eyes that she's already thinking about fucking him. He starts kissing on her and she starts going at him. She's not the type to hold back. They strip each other's clothes off and she's breathing like the fucking has already started.

"Hold on," he says, and runs, dick on pole, out his door and into Quint's room. He opens the top drawer of the dresser and moves Quint's boxers, old jock strap and some Little League baseball socks with the fake stirrups painted on them out of the way so he can see if there are condoms. In the very back there's a one dollar bill. *Good thing you hid yourself some emergency cash*, Marcus thinks. Broke ass nigga. He feels around back there and finds a Durex condom. Thank God. He sneaks back into his room and is glad that Charles, who's home, isn't near enough to see him.

When he comes in, she's laying on her back with her knees in the air. As he walks up, her knees fall to the side like the automatic doors at the grocery store and her shaven pussy sits waiting for company. He puts the condom on, climbs on top and puts himself inside her. She's wet and breathing hard and every pump feels amazing. He loves it that she loves it.

"Give it to me," she whispers. He feels her warm breath on his face and it makes it feel even better. "Fuck that pussy. Oh shit! Oooo! Give me that hard dick. Yeah!" Marcus is giving it to her. Everything he has. And before he knows it, he's gonna come. He pulls out to give it a few seconds to rest and settle down but uh oh, he can't stop it. He tries to flex his dick like he does to stop peeing but it's no use, he pumps six spurts of come out the tip of his dick, into the condom, while he stands on his knees away from her. Fuck, and it didn't even feel good. He puts his dick back in her and resumes the motion.

"Yeah, you like that?" he says.

"Ooo, yeah. Fuck that pussy," she says, but it doesn't sound the same as it did a minute before. He thrusts away, her breath irritating his cheek, and now his dick is getting softer and softer.

"I know you not done already?" she says.

"Yeah, we gotta go. We gotta meet Lenny at the station," he says as he lifts his dick out, holding onto the condom so it doesn't just slide off into her. The tip of his dick is now about an inch below the tip of the condom. He takes it off, ties the end in a knot and throws it in the trash.

"Damn, nigga, what happened to you? I know I got the killer pussy but really? That was about two minute," Tasha says as she starts getting dressed.

"Ay. A nigga's been out of practice. You ain't called me up in over a month," Marcus smiles. "I break you off later on though, don't worry about that."

"Naaaaaa," she says, rolling her eyes. "You seem like you more the one-and-done type to me. I ain't never seen you go more than one round."

"Please." Marcus grabs his notebook, goes and gets a Doral off Charles, and they head out.

They share the cigarette on their walk to the station. Tasha doesn't have any money so Marcus uses the two dollars he was saving for the trip home to pay for her. After what just happened, that's the least he could do. Lenny's not there when they arrive, but they get on the next southbound train anyway. Marcus notices Deon sitting a few seats away with a backpack on. Last time he saw Deon, he was hustling. "Ay, Deon! What's up bruh, you back in school? That trap life too crazy for you, huh?"

"That trap life too boring!" he smiles. "I ain't the type of nigga that could just stand on a corner, all day, every day. Felt like a bus stop and shit." He shakes his head.

"I hear that, bruh. Do your thing." Marcus and Tasha take their seats.

When they get to the house, they walk past two kids playing video games before they reach the studio.

"Tasha!" Lil Kenny says as they enter the studio. "What's up mama?"

"What's up with it, Special K?"

Kenny turns his quick-moving head to Marcus. "I ain't seen this girl in more than a month and she still gonna talk shit right when she see me!"

"It's just 'cause you special to me. You my special K," Tasha says—sometimes her jokes are not that funny.

"Anyway, my nigga, where Lenny?"

"He'll be here in a minute. I don't know how we're gonna do this shit without T, but whatever," Marcus says, and then starts mumbling some lyrics he's been thinking about. "My style'll make you twitch… like a paper cut, slittin' the tip of your dick, dog… I get hard, soft, dro…"

"What, bruh?" Kenny says with a grimace. "Why would you rap about, like…"

"But don't that make you twitch? When you think about a paper cut on the tip of your thang, bruh?"

"I don't know. Maybe. But even if it do, why would you think about something like that," Kenny says. In the next room, the two kids playing video games, who must be friends of Mike's son because they're about ten years old, are starting to raise their voices. Kenny starts walking over to tell them to quiet down.

"Nigga, that's why I seen yo daddy picking up trash at the train station," the tall boy says to the shorter, bigger kid.

"So what, nigga, my daddy say he do whatever he gotta do so we could eat good food every day."

"Nigga yo daddy must be trash man of the year the way yo fatass be eatin."

"Nigga least I ain't eating bread and water like yo daddy up in jail."

"Fuck you, nigga, I don't let nobody talk shit about my daddy," the taller boy says and swings at the fatter boy. They start throwing wild punches as Kenny walks up.

"Ay!" Kenny steps between them and easily throws each kid to the side. "Cut that shit out, y'all in somebody house, have some respect." The fat boy has his face scrunched up and is crying.

"Man, you a little cry baby," the tall boy says.

"Nigga shut yo ass up, everybody cries sometimes, nigga. I seen you cry yesterday," he says with his chin high and a big frown, eyes squinting, and cheeks wet.

"I'ma kick both a y'all out if you don't stop fighting like some little girls. You heard me?"

"Yes," says the short one.

"You heard me? You gonna stop?" Kenny yells at the other boy.

"Yes," he says, looking down at the floor.

"Now we in there trying to rap. Am I gonna hear either one of y'all through that door?"

"No."

"No."

"Alright. I bet not," Kenny goes back into the studio room and shuts the door. One minute after he shuts it, Lenny opens it and walks in.

"How'd y'all get here so fast?" Lenny asks Marcus and Tasha. "I thought y'all might of had some intimate time."

"We did," Tasha says, rolling her eyes—she's never believed in privacy. "Or I should say *he* did."

"Damn, bruh, you quick," Lenny says.

"I take this music shit serious, my nigga, we paying for studio time. Time is money, my nigga," Marcus says.

"Riiiiiiight," Tasha says.

"Can we get back on track?" Marcus says, not wanting to talk about his pitiful sex experience. He flips through his booklet and finds some bars he wrote down. "Ay, you know how everybody got some type of fix that they gotta have though, right? Like some niggas need to smoke weed every day. Some gotta have they cigarettes. And some people, you don't *think* they got a fix, but then guess what, they be drinking coffee or like five sodas a day, right?"

"Drinking liquor, too," Kenny says.

"How'd I know you was gonna say that? Alcoholic-ass nigga," Marcus continues. "So this one right here like… it's like:
What's your fix? What's your fix? What's, your fucking fix?/
What's the shit that make you tick/
If you can't cop it you can't drop it/
What's your fix? What's your fix? What's, your motherfucking fix?
And then it's like,
I'm a fiend for the nicotine/

Gotta have that caffeine/
Weed on my lunch break/
Gotta have that visine.
And then it's like,
You got addicts of all kinds/
What's your fix I'll tell you mines/
For the body or the mind/
Or maybe just to pass the time."

They work on the track for a few more minutes, talking about whether the hook is too simple or if it's good because sometimes simple means it's more catchy. Kenny sits on a stool with his right leg twitching. He works on a verse about green, since he's high:

"I love to smoke dro. Shit, I can't lie/
Half the deep thoughts, I get, is when I'm high/
It helps me relax/
It helps me chill out/
It helps me keep a level head/
When the world wile' out."

"Cool let's do it," says Marcus. "We only got a half hour left. Let's get those beats together and lay some shit down." They record as many of Tasha's vocals as they can since they don't know the next time she'll be there.

Lenny grabs the mic while it's recording, gets his eyes really big, and starts talking: "It feels good to be at the top of the top. I'm at the point where I'm so fucking hot that I get paid for anything that comes out my mouth. Matter a fact, anything that comes outta me, period. I could take a shit on this microphone, and mufuckas'll pay to hear it. Mufuckas'll pay to hear me even talk about taking a shit on a microphone. Like right now, mufuckas will probably pay for this shit—hearing me talk about talking about taking a shit on a microphone… shit is crazy—I never thought I would get this famous."

"You got the best imagination—I give you that," Lil' Kenny says, and they pack their shit up and go home.

Chapter 26 – Quintavious

"Here's what it is. It's gonna be guys that wanna fuck you and it's gonna be girls that wanna fuck me—that's just a reality—and I know that. We can't help that—alls we can help is how we deal with them. I've been in relationships before and it's about trust," Quint says to Ramona through the cordless phone. He's on his bed with his arm on Drama and his leg resting on Dora. He considers saying that there's also going to be people that *he* wants to fuck and people that *she* wants to fuck, but decides some things are better left unsaid.

"I don't feel comfortable committing to only one person," she says. "I'm sorry. I care about you and I want to continue seeing you but I just don't believe in monogamy."

Damn—so she doesn't want to leave anything to the imagination—she doesn't only want to admit that she wants to fuck other guys, she wants to actually fuck other guys. He ain't never heard a female just come right out and say it like that. All of a sudden he feels a million miles away from her. Like he doesn't know her. Like he's talking to a telemarketer trying to sell him some shit to the point where he almost just feels like hanging up on her. But shit, might as well just ask her straight up. "So you wanna fuck other guys?"

"I don't know," she says. "It doesn't have anything to do with how I feel about you. I like you. I might even love you. I haven't felt this excited for a relationship in a long time." Quint hears the word love, but doesn't know how to take it. "It's just that I don't believe people should be possessive of each other so I don't want someone controlling who I can be intimate with. Does that make sense?" she says, but nothing makes sense. And the fact that she is asking him *does it make sense* gets on his nerves. He used to think it was cute—like the white people way of saying *you feel me*— but now it was like she was talking down to him like he was a dumbass. Does it make sense… Bitch, of course it makes sense—it's not like you're saying anything complicated. "And I want you to be happy," she continues. "You can have sex with whoever you want."

He *should* be happy. She just said she loved him and he can fuck whoever he wants. What more could you ask for? But he's not—all he can do is picture Ramona with other men and he can't shake the feeling—it spreads all throughout his insides. Is he wrong for feeling that? Is he just hung up on how men are supposed to want to control women? That's what she would say. She would say being free to be with other people is the more natural way but that society has brainwashed us to be possessive of each other. Maybe he just needs to get over it. Maybe that's it. And it would be cool to be able to just call up another girl and have it be all good with Ramona. Damn… It ain't really no option but to take the high road. "It's cool with me if it's cool with you. I like being with you—I'm not even interested in nobody else right now."

"Me too!" It's obvious that she is excited that he's on board with the plan. And maybe she just wants the option to be with someone else, but she won't actually do it as long as they're doing cool.

"So you leave tomorrow morning for the protest thing?"

"Yeah we're taking two vans. You sure you don't want to come?"

"Stop playing. What I look like in a tie dye shirt trying to protest some shit? They for sure arrest my ass just for looking out of place."

"Okay first of all I'm definitely getting you a tie dye shirt for a souvenir. Second of all, we're demonstrating against the Western Hemisphere Institute for Security Cooperation and it has nothing to do with wearing tie dye."

"Against the who about the what?" He gives an ugly look to the phone and then puts it back on his ear.

"It's a school that the U.S. runs that trains people from Latin America to be dictators and pawns for the U.S. They train them up here and then they send them back down to run their countries based on what the U.S. wants."

"I'll take your word for it," Quint says. He feels like asking her why she always wants to protest some shit that is happening in other states and around the world when there's so much shit going on here, but decides to just wish her well and leave it at that.

Chapter 27 – Nick

It's the third time Nick's given Luana a ride home from work. He's in his regular place at her apartment, which is pacing around her bedroom, drinking a Bacardi and Coke. The drinks have gotten stronger and stronger with each visit.

"You're trying to get me drunk aren't you?" he says.

"Maybe." He walks over and asks her what she's having. She's standing in front of the fridge, and while he asks her, he brushes his hand across her lower back. "Bloody Mary," she says.

"Right on," he says, and sits at the little kitchen table. "Hey, you know my friend from school is Marcus's brother's girlfriend? Me and Marcus just figured that out today."

"What do you mean your friend? Like what kind of friend?" she asks.

"My friend. Marcus's brother's girlfriend," Nick says. Did she really just say that? They drink their drinks and listen to Sublime—Nick notices that she usually puts on white music. Then he thinks about how he usually puts on black music. They talk about high school, and Luana tells him about her long relationship with an older dude from age fifteen to nineteen. The guy was six years older than she was.

"That's fucked up," Nick says.

"He hit me one final time and I unloaded six rounds at his ass. Didn't hit the bastard but he ran the hell out of there," she does her Beavis and Butthead laugh as she drags her cigarette.

He wonders if the old dude was black and if that might be the reason why she likes white guys now. Whatever. Who cares. He finishes his drink and she pours him another one. This one's so potent it tastes like Coke-flavored rum. It even smells like straight liquor, so he holds his breath as he drinks. Damn, she's gonna force him to make a move, he thinks, getting him all drunk and looking so good in those tight black pants—she looks like a miniature Rihanna from the Umberella video. *You could stand under my um-berella, ella, ella, ay, ay, ay...* He whistles the melody with a shshshsh sound that comes off kind of like a tea pot, then walks up to her. "So how do I know you're not gonna unload six rounds on me if we start messing around?" Nick goes over, walks behind her chair, and puts his hands on her shoulders and gives a little massage.

"I don't *mess around*," she says as she walks slowly away from him but looks back in a seductive smile.

"You're right, you're right; it probably won't be anything ever. You have a little boyfriend and everything," he says as he follows her. She stops and turns around, looking into his eyes. His legs stop but he continues to float into her as she lifts her head and reaches her lips up to his. They kiss, and Nick holds her small lower back as she arches up to him. It's delicate and soft, and a little bit thrilling. Not that he would want to ruin their relationship, but the thing is, it's already pretty much failed anyway.

"I shouldn't be doing this," she says like it's her line in a movie. "And now my decision is even harder."

"Your decision's harder?" Nick says.

"I was hoping you'd be a bad kisser so I wouldn't want to do anything with you."

Nick goes back to his chair, grabs his glass, and tries to finish his stiff-ass drink. "But seriously, you need to make a decision to either end it with him or stop talking to me."

"How do you think it would end up with *us*?" she asks, in a suddenly sober voice. "Because I don't want to start anything that's not going to end up as something."

"I think it would first be love. And I think it would end up with a baby in a baby carriage. No, I don't know—who knows how anything's gonna turn out?"

"Okay you can leave now."

"No I was just joking around."

"And why did you leave out marriage? First comes love, then comes *marriage*."

"Legal prostitution? Selling out your freedom so the government can tell you how to have a relationship?" He had just had this conversation with Ramona.

"Okay you can definitely leave now. I would never have a child out of wedlock—you won't find me as a single mom."

"Fine—I do! I do! I'll marry you."

"Be serious," she says quietly.

"Ok, but isn't this talk supposed to come after you've been having sex with someone for like six months?"

"You're the one who brought it up."

Women are crazy.

Nick goes up to her and faces her, holding the sides of her stomach. She really might be the one. "I think this is gonna work—I really like you." He kisses her. "You need to go talk to him."

"I might do it tomorrow," she says.

"Also, it's important to sleep with someone so you see how you connect on that level. So I would say it might not be a bad idea to have sex just so we know what the chemistry level is, you know what I mean?"

"You would say that," Luana says, trying not to smile. "I *might* talk to him tomorrow—if you're lucky."

"I am, actually, really lucky," he says.

Chapter 28 – Marcus

Marcus sees Nick take like a full minute to clock back in after lunch.

"What's up my Nicka?" he says. He's felt bad ever since he found out the pizza boy was Nick's brother.

Nick gives a head nod and slowly grabs a work order from the wall, checks it out, and then puts it back and grabs an easy "RESTROOM" vinyl sign on aluminum that needs to be made. Charles follows him with his eyes. "Okay, I've seen all three of y'all pick up that work order and then put it back. If you guys don't try to do every type of sign, I'm telling you, you're never gonna learn and Gary's gonna see it and fire your ass. He's already looking for reasons to get rid of you and I bet you somebody gets fired this month 'cause if y'all make it past this month then he has to pay your unemployment. Matter of fact, knowing Gary, he'll probably get rid of two of y'all.

"Why you so scary? Man, fuck Gary," Marcus says.

"I ain't scared of nobody. I'm trying to give y'all some advice. You do whatever you wanna do, though."

"I'll learn that shit tomorrow. I'm too high right now," Nick says.

"Man I *knew* this man was high. Nick, man, how you gon do me like that, man. You just gon leave and not tell a nigga you smoking."

"My fault," Nick says, looking high as hell.

"I bet that shit was some bomb, too! Them white boys be smoking that sticky icky. Huh, Nick? That must have been some purp or something. Huh, Nick? That dro?"

"It was good," Nick says slowly, trying to flex his cheek muscles to stop a grin.

"That's that good right there. Damn, you wrong for that!"

Julio looks up. "Ay Nick, what'd you smoke out of? One of them glass pipes? Or a doobee—them white boys be rollin' them pinner ass joints, fool—doobees. Huh, Nick?"

Nick looks up from his work and his eyes are slits. "A bong," he says, and Marcus and Julio almost fall over laughing. Charles is laughing too.

"This man said a bong, dog! Hell naw," Marcus says, trying to catch his breath. "On the lunch break, too."

Finally Charles makes them shut up when the Isley Brothers come on the radio and they work quietly for a couple minutes until

Julio breaks the silence. "Ay, fool, if you was gay would you be the one fucking or would you be the one getting fucked?" he says.

"I'm cool, bruh—I wouldn't do either one."

"I be the one fuckin, dog!" Julio says and they all start busting up again, until Gary walks in.

"Charles I need you and Julio to go do an install at Tony's pizza. It shouldn't take more than forty-five minutes, is that clear?" Gary says.

"Yeah, we got it." Charles turns to Julio. "Get two blades, some scissors, Windex, a squeegee, a level, and some paper towels and meet me outside." Charles gets the work order and walks out to the van.

Gary walks around the huge table to each person's workstation. "This table looks like shit. How many times do I have to tell you guys to put the materials back after you're done. And Marcus, son, what the hell is this? Have you ever seen a DO NOT ENTER sign with a white background?" Gary waits but it's not clear if he wants him to say something or not, so Marcus just looks at the sign. He didn't notice anything wrong with it, really. "NO—it's red! That's because it's a reverse sign. You weed off the letters instead of the background." Gary pounds his fist on the table.

"It never said that," Marcus says.

"Where's the work order? Let's look at the fucking work order," Gary says, his face pink like bubble gum. Marcus looks around the table for the work order. "Do you guys ever read the work order? What do you think it's for? It's so you don't fuck up the sign and cost me money!" Marcus finds the little work order bag with the sketch and information in it. Gary rips it out and slams it on the table. "You see that? What does that say?"

"Reverse. Nobody ever told me about reverse though."

"I'm sick of these excuses. Son, your problem is that you don't listen. I'm done with you. Go clock out. Get the hell out of here."

"I'll do it over again—it's the first time I seen one like that," Marcus says, on his way to pick up another sheet of aluminum—this motherfucker can't fire him over one little mistake; he must be playing.

"If you have anything in the back room, get it, and clock out. You're done working at RapidSigns, son."

"Let me work till the end of the week at least, Gary. I need the money."

Gary sits down at his computer against the wall of the production room. "Son," he says into the screen, "you're on private property—you need to get out of my store before I call the police."

"Call the police?" Marcus says. Shit—he for sure ain't getting his job back now. "Call the police, then! You old fat, scary motherfucker. You need the police 'cause I know you not gonna do nothing yourself. Probably have a heart attack, fat-ass, alcoholic-punk-motherfucker." Gary's trying to show no emotion—just sitting at his desk staring forward. "I just feel bad for you. Only reason your wife fucks you 'cause you got money, you fat fuck."

"At least I have a job. Get the hell out!" Gary says and picks up his desk phone. "Yes we have a disruptive employee that just got fired and is trespassing and refusing to leave," Gary says. "Okay. Thank you." He hangs up.

Instead of leaving, Marcus walks right up to where Gary is sitting. He stands one foot away from him and stares down at his big head and big eyes and big red face. "Hey boy," Marcus says, talking to Gary the way *he* talks to *him*. "Hey, son. Look at me when I speak to you. Matter of fact, keep staring at that computer like the scary fat fuck that you is." He glances over to give Nick a quick nod—Nick gives a nervous smile and shakes his head. "That's what I thought," Marcus looks like he's about to spit on Gary, then starts walking out of the production room to the front office.

"You done now? Get the hell out of my store," Gary says, trying to get the last word in. But Marcus stops. Turns. And then runs back into the room and right up to Gary, who starts backing up. "Lu-ANNA! Lu-ANNA!" he cries. Marcus reaches back with his right arm, lines up Gary's face, starts to let it fly and then completely stops halfway through the right hook, turns back around and leaves the sign shop, laughing.

"Alright then Nick, I holler at you," he says as he steps out the door. He laughs as he thinks about the scared look on Gary's face, and then his smile drops. It drops one hundred percent. And he feels like a fuck-up. Like a fuck-up that can't keep a job. Like he shouldn't even have gotten it in the first place.

Back to no money.

And even now, he doesn't have a dollar in his pocket, so he walks home. Charles is going to get on him for this. But he only messed up two signs. Most of his signs looked good, and plus, Charles told him that all that vinyl shit is cheap as hell. Gary makes a killing on every sign, even if you have to re-do it five times. That's how cheap the materials are.

Marcus is a few blocks from home and is calculating how much his last paycheck is going to be when he sees Franky and his girl walking by. Franky went to school with Marcus at West Side High and Marcus knows that Franky is from the 100's. Those boys from the 100s and niggas from the 90s don't get along.

"Y'all better get on," Marcus says, trying to let them know that it's not safe for them around these blocks. Franky's girlfriend looks pregnant, too.

"Nigga I'm walking my girl home. I'll walk wherever the fuck I needa walk."

"Go ahead. You do what you wanna do," Marcus says, and keeps walking. He's not sure if someone heard them or what, but up about a block he sees five of his boys from 96th talking shit to Franky. They about to whoop his ass. Normally he'd go over and get in the mix. And not because he's scared, but he's just in a sad mood like fuck it, so he decides to walk straight to his apartment.

He walks in and Dora and Drama wag their tails and show him some love. He sits on the couch and flips the TV on. Mama's not home yet so he taps the couch with his hand—both dogs jump up and curl into balls against the end of the couch. Marcus scrunches into them and uses Dora as a warm pillow. His heart is still beating fast from the encounter with Gary, but Dora's relaxed breathing beneath Marcus's head slows him into a peaceful nap.

Chapter 29 – Quintavious

As Quint sees the 42 coming down Patriot, he can't shake his dream from out his head. Actually, not the whole dream—he can't even remember the whole dream—but that last part—the part when Ramona gave him that look. She came around the corner of some big, fancy, all white tent-like thing, and gave him a look that hit deep, like a gut punch. The rest of the dream is a blur, but that look—her big eyes still and serious, staring through his eyes and down into his stomach.

He remembers that. But why did a look hurt so much? They hadn't even been talking during the dream and he wasn't close to her, maybe twenty feet away, but it might as well have been from a thousand feet away—that's how distant she seemed in the dream. And that was part of why it hurt—because he felt so distant.

He goes back and forth between trying to shake Ramona's death look from out his head and trying to recall the rest of the dream. Fuck, he hates how he can never remember dreams. Marcus remembers all his dreams, but he ain't never been able to do it.

The bus squeaks to a halt and Quint steps on, peels off a couple one dollar bills from the thin fold of cash in his pocket, and then presses them into the receptacle. The bus is about half full with people headed towards downtown. He takes an open seat across the aisle from a dark skinned girl reading a biology textbook.

Quint lifts a finger and nods in her direction. "Ay, you know where the, umm, post office is? The downtown one?" That was one thing that T taught him—if you want to talk to females, you gotta say some shit right away—it don't really matter what you say, you just gotta say something—you can't wait around in silence for a half an hour before you talk—then you just come off like a creepy motherfucker.

She looks up from her book. "It should be one on Adams Street that's closer."

"Oh, okay. Cool. Yeah I gotta send a letter," Quint says, and as the words leave his mouth, he questions the quality of his game.

"Where you from?" she says.

"Why? I got a accent or something?"

She looks out the window.

"Why? For real?" Quint repeats, fake smiling.

"Didn't you just ask me where the post office is?"

"Oh shit!" he says, real smiling. "Yeah. Naw, I'm from here—and you right, I *should* know where it is, but you know how they keep moving it and everything."

"Whatever they ain't never moved that post office. My grandma been going there her whole life."

"Yeah, that's true," Quint says. "Damn, you don't let a nigga get away with nothing, huh? I bet your man says 'I'm tired' and you be like, 'no you ain't, prove it.'"

She finally smiles. "Whatever—that ain't true."

Quint switches his legs into the aisle. "You go to City College?"

"Yeah this my last class till I can go to the nursing school," she says, and sounds so sweet and honest. You can tell by her voice that she's doing things the right way. And for all the bullshitting he's doing, she just sounds so honest and hardworking.

"That's what I should be doing," he says. "I mean, not nursing, but…"

"You know what though? You'd be surprised—it's a lot of guy nurses nowadays—they even want more guy nurses—and they make that same salary. Shoot."

"Quintavious—the man nurse," he laughs. She smiles as she unwraps a stick of gum and offers Quint one.

"That's a pretty name."

"First you want me to be a nurse and now you saying I'm pretty—you really trying to get me to bring out my feminine side, ain't you?"

"I'm Anika," she says. She's so calm and collected, about her business but still caring—not trying to front to nobody. She for sure must have a man. They're getting near the stop and Quint is thinking about getting that number but he also just can't stop thinking about his dream. And Ramona.

"Let me ask you something," he says. She rotates to him—their knees within a foot of each other. "So I'm in this relationship, right?"

"Um hmm," she says, like *here we go again—another disloyal black man.*

"And I know it's gonna sound crazy, but the way *we* do things, and just hear me out, the way *we* believe in things—is that it's better to have a open relationship where you could see other people. So you don't hold the other person back, you feel me? It ain't none of that controlling, where you been, who you been with, let me look through your phone… Everybody just free. Like, it's the ultimate freedom, you feel me?" He says, and tries to figure out how she's gonna respond. Sistahs for sure ain't down with this type of thing, but Quint is ready to defend his point.

"I feel you," she says, like she's fully on board.

"Huh?! For real?"

"I'm sick of niggas cheating, lying, trying to cover shit up. Shoot—at least this way everybody could just be honest and it ain't like one person creeping and the other just getting played for the fool."

Quint sits there, staring at the No Food, Drinks, Cigarettes, or Music sign at the front of the bus. This is not how he predicted the conversation would go. He's not sure he actually believes her. "But like, are you just saying that because you think your man will cheat anyway so you just want him to be honest? Like, what would you rather? A honest man in a open relationship or a honest man in a faithful relationship?"

"I ain't got a man," she says in between chews of gum. "And I ain't gonna lie, like, with all this school and work, I'm not even trying to have a man like that."

And all of a sudden she looks extra sexy. Those lips are glistening and those breasts are stretching her shirt towards him. "We just passed your stop," she says.

Quint looks at her contemplatively. It's actually easier talking to ladies when you already got one, he decides. "You seen that new water fountain they got up there on the north side of downtown at that little park?"

"Water fountain?"

"Like a fountain, with water? Why you playin' you know what I mean." Quint gives her a little side bump with his elbow and hears her cute laugh.

Anika pulls her phone from her purse. "Okay I'll go—I can't be long though," she says.

They stay on the bus until they pass Carnegie station and then get off. It's a good thing Ramona never comes up to this area. Wait, it doesn't matter—he's a free man—he can do whatever he wants.

They keep chatting as they walk by a massage parlor and it hits him—the dream—everything comes back to him and it's like a re-run in his head—so powerful that he can't hardly pay attention to Anika.

He's in one of them huge wedding tents, and he walks in and it's like harps and flutes and pianos playing. Two hundred massage tables spaced perfectly in rows and beautiful women standing next to them. It's guys too, but it's like he doesn't even see the guys—all he sees is the ladies. Every complexion and culture is there.

And it's like he knows Ramona is there somewhere, but he's not worried about her. He goes to his table and lays down and get the most sensual and beautiful touch of his life. The woman feels him and she knows him and there's not one ounce of anything wrong and they rub each other and she comes onto the table with him and they keep going all the way to the end and when it ends they lay there and they don't say anything and he gets up and gets his towel and he's feeling so magnificent and he walks to the pool that is outside and then he sees her. Ramona. From a distance. And that's when she gives him the look and it hits him… and he's giving her a look too because he knows she knows what went down with him and so she's giving him a look and she knows that he knows what went down with her and so he's giving her a look.

Quint snaps back to the present and finds himself sitting at the fountain, alone. He stands and prepares to leave, feels an urge to leave right away, when he sees the biology book sitting next to him. His stomach rises. Anika appears from the restroom and he wants to dip. He doesn't know what to say and he doesn't want to deal with it, he just wants to go. He can still make it without her seeing him if he leaves towards the back of the park, so he begins walking. And then he sees himself doing what he hates— running from everything. And he remembers when he fought through it with Ramona—when she was about to leave and he didn't let her, he stood up for himself because he knew he couldn't keep running away from everything. But Anika ain't shit—he just met her.

He leaves behind the other side of the bathroom so she can't see him. He feels like a bitch for not even paying her the respect of saying goodbye. Why would he act one way with a white girl and not the same way with a black girl? Damn, damn, damn.

Chapter 30 – Nick

"You really told him?" Nick says into the phone. "So you guys are done. Finished. Phillip's gonna move on with his little life." He squats down, wearing only a white collared shirt, until his ball sack hairs touch the floor, and then springs into a jump kick.

He lets Luana know that he'll be there in forty-five minutes and that the white linen party has an indoor pool and an open bar. She says, "Thanks baby." The first time she's called him that. He gets a small erection.

His white pants are laid out on a towel on the floor, and he wishes he hadn't swiped the iron from his mom and had just asked to borrow it, because she would have definitely reminded him about getting the ironing board to go along with it.

After getting dressed, he climbs onto the toilet to see his entire outfit in the mirror. She better watch out tonight. Bright white everything—pants, shirt, shoes, even belt. Thrifty Thrift comes through again! A few sprays of Cool Water cologne and he's ready to go.

Eighty bucks for the night, so he should be all right if he plays it right. But it's too cold and wet out to walk— and his steering is still fucked up from when he dodged that chipmunk and hit the mailbox— so he calls a taxi and tells them to meet him outside the gas station.

After dodging raindrops for a couple blocks, he gets to the Citgo. The place is packed. Nick takes his place in line, and looks at their cigarettes. Those Dorals are tempting, still on promotion price for four bucks, but shit, this is a first date—better go with the Marlboro Lights. Nick's right leg is shaking like he has Parkinson's because the jackass at the front of the line has to get fifteen different scratchers from the display case. He tells himself to calm down, there's plenty of time, but that doesn't work, he's still shaking, so he decides to take a survey in his head to pass the time. He counts off the first ten guys he sees. On his left hand, he tallies the ones he imagines have bigger dicks than him. On his right, smaller. 6-4. Not bad—he's bigger than 40%. In the 40th percentile. That's about average—he'll take it. God damn would these people please hurry the fuck up? He sees his cab pull up and signals for him to wait, then finally makes his transaction and gets in the car.

The driver asks Nick where he's going, a KKK rally? Nick asks him where he's coming from, the twin towers? They laugh and Nick gets dropped off at the package store so he can buy some

Crown and a liter of Pepsi. He looks at his money as he walks out—forty bucks left.

The rain stops and the final six blocks go by in a hurry. He slows down before getting to her apartment—doesn't want to be out of breath. And if he didn't already know she likes him, he'd duck behind a bush and take a couple swigs of the whiskey—but there's no need for that.

He walks up her dark wooden stairway and knocks on the cracked open door. The beautiful fragrance of girl lifts him as she opens the door—burning tea candles carefully scattered around the room transform it into something out of a movie, or like an IKEA room. He must have done something good to get to be here right now.

"I like everything you did around here," Nick says, wiggling a finger at the room. Then he nods at Luana. "And what you did right there."

"Are you saying I look beautiful?" she says, like she's teaching him how to express himself. "Thanks, baby. And look at you! I'm impressed. I didn't think you could pull it off." Nick's found that if you pay top dollar at a good thrift shop, you can get quality shit at a good price.

"You don't know a lot of things about me," Nick says. She takes the bottle of Crown out of the purple velvet and Nick stops her, insisting on making the drinks while she finishes getting ready. Everything's right on track.

They drink a couple stiff ones and then get in the cab and are on their way. They get to the block it's on and Nick gets out to find the party. He runs up slate walkways, lined with ivy, looking for address numbers, lights, movement—any sign of the white linen party.

He peels off fingernail tips with his teeth as he jogs back to the cab and lets himself in. He waits for her to speak.

"You can't find it?"

"I found it all right." He looks at her with raised eyebrows, then pokes some air out of his nose. "And when I walked in, guess what else I found? Two of my exes, sitting by the pool. I'm *not* dealing with that tonight.

"I wanna go to the party," she says in a quiet, pouty voice. "Fuck those bitches—I'll beat their asses."

"Baby—you're not going to *beat* anyone's ass." Did she really just say that? And did he really just call her baby? "I'm sorry." He puts his hand on her leg and gives her thigh a little squeeze. "Can we just go somewhere else?"

She squints at him.

He goes in for a kiss.

She retracts her head. "Make-up," she says.

Damn.

If a white girl said that, he'd think she was stuck up, but with Luana, it just makes him want to kiss her more. "Let's go to Après Diem," she says.

"She's the boss," Nick says loudly to the cabby and they take off back to the Community to a bourgie bar that Nick's never been to. He lifts the bills in his pocket to see what he's down to—shit— thirty bucks. He asks Luana what she wants as she heads to the bathroom.

"Bombaby Sapphire martini, extra dirty," she says. *Bombay Sapphire martini extra dirty, Bombay Sapphire martini extra dirty—he* memorizes the tongue twister as he gets the bar tender's attention and then orders the drink. "And for me, whiskeycoke." Nick looks back towards the restroom and realizes Luana's still in there. He leans over the bar. "Matter a fact, bro, use the well liquor for that martini—she won't know the difference."

He gathers the drinks and then snags a black leather love seat next to a glass table. He waits impatiently. The large, spread out venue hasn't filled up yet, but there are quite a few couples sprinkled around, settling into their dates. Most of them are white—she *would* choose a place like that. He takes a quick sip of her drink for taking too long. He taps his feet on the floor, his fingers on the table, and then does the dick survey again to bide some time.

Finally she joins him and they sink into the cushions, drinking their drinks. "Why didn't you let me see your ex-girlfriends?"

"Trust me, it would *not* have been a pretty scene." Why is she talking about this?

"I'm asking you why. You thought we would fight?"

"No—she's not like that… they're not like that."

"You can't handle more than one girl at a time?" she says. He rotates his glass three times and then takes a large pull. "Good drink?" she says, seeing him tongue tied. "And for the record, I only do threesomes in the first month I date someone. After that, it gets awkward—I don't like to share. So if you're interested, you might want to get on it." She sits up, back straight, crosses her legs and takes the olive in her front lips and then bites off half. *She knows exactly what she's doing.*

"Yeah," he says. "I'm on it." She's the one. She really might be the one. "But…" he lifts both hands in front of him and shakes them like he has epilepsy. "Slow down. I haven't even agreed to sleep with *you* yet. And you're talking about bringing in friends? This is our first date—remember. Don't think I'm gonna just throw off my pants."

She turns her body to him and then moves her mouth towards his. He guides his lips until they nearly touch, then sharply retracts his head. "Chap stick," he says, and points to his lips.

She pulls his shirt and then slightly opens her mouth, giving him a lick-kiss to preserve her lipstick. He follows suit, at the same time enjoying the delicate touch of tongue and also resisting the urge to pull her body into his.

Luana buys a round and then Nick buys a round and then Luana buys a round. Nick's broke.

"Do you only date white guys?" he asks.

"I like white boys," she says, and does her Beavis and Butthead laugh. Nick wonders if she's only with him because he's white, but decides to think about that later, when he's sober. "I was on the bus today and was talking to this white guy," she continues, "and these black guys were trying to get at me and wanted me to come to the back. After I told them that I was in the middle of a conversation and it's rude to interrupt, they kept talking so I had to cuss them out." She smiles.

"Let's go," Nick says, full of energy and in the perfect comfort zone.

"Night cap? My place?" she says. They walk out into the cold, wet night.

"Just remember my policy about the first night and everything and don't try to get in my pants, all right?" he says.

"In your dreams," she says. "Remember when I told you you can't handle this?" she says, and then lifts the left side of her top with her right hand and pulls it down, bra included, so that her breast is exposed. She looks up at him while pointing her tongue toward the nipple, and then starts cracking up.

"Remember when I told you…" he starts, but isn't sure where he's going with the sentence, "that you can't handle *this*?" he says, and then glances down at the front of his pants.

"I'm sorry. I don't understand. That I can't handle what?" she says.

"You'd like to know, huh?"

"Hurry up and call a cab, pretty boy," she says. He knows he only has a few dollars left though.

"I kind of feel like walking—it's just so nice, and cold, out."

"I'm paying—call a cab," she says. Nick calls a cab and they go back to Luana's.

They walk in. She wobbles back and forth and her eyes are struggling to focus. "I'm gonna make you a special drink," she says with a sloppy smile as she pushes and then pulls open the bathroom door.

"Special drink from the bathroom?" Nick says, looking at the door. He hears her gag. "Baby!" he yells. He likes the sound of it. He loves the sound of it. He loves her. He's finally found his queen. "You want some water?" She doesn't answer.

In the kitchen, he turns the faucet on full and takes ten swallows down the throat like a keg stand. He strips down his white layers and waits for her in bed. Waits to hold her. It will feel so good to hold her. He tries to wait. He tries, but falls into commercial dreams, his mind flashing from random thing to the next.

Hours go by. He dreams of crawling through a tunnel, searching for the White Linen party. And then he hears a ring tone. The ring moves from his dream to his real life, waking him up. He sees Luana sitting up in bed with a serious look on her face.

"Phillip," she says into her phone.

Nick's eyes open.

"No. You can't."

Her eyes dart from Nick back to the phone. "It's not a good time. I have company," she says.

Then footsteps. Loud thuds up a wooden staircase. Nick's chest raises and he blinks his eyes rapidly, like the blurry picture just needs to be focused. He looks towards her door and watches as it flies open. There he stands. Phillip. Her boyfriend. Her ex-boyfriend. Red, sweaty skin and lively eyes. He searches the space, like he's even surprised himself that the door was unlocked and that he actually made it in.

"What the fuck are you doing? That's my fucking girl!" Phillip says. Nick is sitting on the bed but makes no attempt to stand. "No no no no no no, you don't understand, that's my fucking girl." It's like it's a movie. Like he's acting. There's something about the words that are coming out of his mouth that sound fake. Phillip turns to Luana. "Baby, what are you doing?" Now he's calling her Baby, too. "I *love* you. We're supposed to be together.

Nick lifts his bunched white pants from the floor and pulls them on his skinny legs. He feels for his cigarettes and then lights one.

"Bro," Nick says as he exhales. "Are you really doing this right now? You're being serious right now?"

Phillip looks at Nick, then back at Luana. "You left me for his skinny ass?"

Now Nick kind of wants to fight him.

"Phillip, you need to go," Luana finally says. And then nothing more. Does she even give a fuck?

Hungover, drunk… this rude awakening is worse than when Alex used to put his bare ass on Nick's face and fart. "Bro, did I ever come over here when you guys were going out?"

"We *are* going out! She's not with you. Get it in your head. She's entertaining you because she's mad at me. It's a game. Tell him, Baby. Tell him.

Nick sucks on the Marlboro Light. He reviews the events slowly and clearly. Man 1 runs in on man 2 with woman. Man 1 tries to win woman back.

There is no decision to make. The next move is clear. He needs to fight him. And in order to fight him, he needs to use the magic word. "You're acting like a bitch running in here at six in the morning." It's not really true, but it doesn't matter if it's true or not, Nick has known the power of the b word ever since he saw Alex call Mom a bitch and she slapped the shit out of him. But he had not used it for three weeks because Ramona said men shouldn't use it. Ever. But this is a different situation. He needs to fight for his respect and he needs to fight for his relationship. He watches Phillip and it's almost like you can see the gears turning in his head. And then he snaps into motion. He comes rushing at Nick like a mad fourth grader—arms extended, before Nick is able to do anything. Nick can't get a punch off before both their bodies slam to the floor. Nick's on bottom and Phillip tries to swing at Nick's face, but Nick holds him close enough so he can't get the proper extension. Nick needs to free himself and escape Phillip's weight. They roll around, Phillip holding on and Nick pushing away.

He throws his elbow into Phillip's side and scoots out from under him. They launch over to the foot of Luana's bed, battling for the offensive. They swing and block and swing and block. Phillip comes with a right hook and catches Nick's lip before he slips onto his knees. Nick grabs his blond fro in his left hand and swings away at his skull with his right. Phillip's head is right over Nick's crotch. Phillip tries to jerk away with his neck but Nick's fingers, forearm, and bicep allow his head to go nowhere. He swings again at Phillip's head but fatigue is setting in and the power is dropping fast. The punches to the head are doing nothing. Then he notices his knee brushing against Phillip's chin, so he pulls the fro a couple inches higher and then jerks his knee up as hard as he can… BLAAAW—knee bone to nose, exploding a bloody mess on linen pants and sheets. Fuck. Everything turns into slow motion, like he's watching himself. He's not angry at Phillip. It's like everyone's just playing their roles. He's not mad at Phillip. He doesn't hate him. He's just trying to do the right thing in a fight.

"Cut it out!" Luana unleashes the order and the two perk to attention like teenage lovers getting caught fucking. They stand hunched, hands on knees, panting. Luana has transformed into a drill sergeant. "Phillip—you're sweet, honey, and I love you, but we're done," she says, and gives him a 'welcome to Wal-Mart' fake smile. "Okay?" she adds. He knows it's rhetorical and doesn't respond. "Nick," she says with her chin up so that she can look down on him. "You need help. You're a fucking liar." She pauses. "You dropped out of college. You didn't get kicked out for being a vegetarian. And last night, there was either no party to begin with or you simply just couldn't find the party. No open bar, no ex-girlfriends. Stop lying."

"There was a party to begin with…" Nick says, and then feels like a dumbass for not saying something better.

But he doesn't want to make something up.

Why didn't she say anything to Phillip about busting into her apartment?

"You both need to leave now," she says.

"I'm not leaving till he does," Phillip says, with a trail of blood from his nose down to his chin. Nick pictures his little cousins having to clean up their games—*I'm not picking up the Legos until he does.* He's waiting for Phillip to stomp on the ground when he looks up to see Luana doctoring his face with a wet paper towel. He wonders if it's broken, and as he watches, he's not sure if he wants Luana to come to him to show him love or continue medicating Phillip's bloody face. Nick puts on his socks and shoes, grabs his shirt and leaves.

As he walks up the sidewalk at what turns out to be only 6:20 a.m., his white button-up is open, chest pulsing. He walks quickly, and for the first block slows his pace three times to retch the contents in his stomach out through his mouth. He doesn't taste any of the dark yellow mixture of Crown Royal, Jim Beam, Pepsi, and bile. His body is too energized to stop completely, so he only slows, leans his torso to the right, and lets it out. He presses his finger to each nostril and shoots snot rockets to the sidewalk. Even though he's a little bit stunned, he is content and relieved. There's something to say about being thrown on your toes—the moments in life when your reactions to every split second are crucial. When God sees if you can come through in the clutch. Sometimes you pray to have a re-try after these events. Now, even though he has no idea what will come of it all, he's happy to accept the event into his past.

He didn't play his hand perfectly, but he played it better than he usually does, and he definitely played it better than Phillip played his.

He drags a forearm across his mouth, smearing a bright red strip along his pale skin. Later it will be dry and dark. What will happen then? When the blood dries. When Phillip's blood dries. Who cares. Luana might be fucking him right now. Whatever. If that's what he needs to do to get some pussy.

Nick passes the package store, crosses the parking lot to Kroger, and goes through the automatic doors past the security guard, who is talking with some friends. "They're gonna make you button that shirt up, sir," he says as Nick walks in. Nick buttons his shirt without a pause in his step. He needs some hydration and he needs something to occupy himself during the walk home, so he grabs a Power Aid and proceeds to the checkout. The cashier acts like she doesn't notice the blood on his shirt and the cut on his lip. He cracks open the cool drink and the blue liquid washes the acid from his mouth back to its rightful place in his stomach. As he exits the grocery store, the security guard's friend speaks to him, "You doing alright, man? You got some blood on you. Somebody got you?"

"Something like that," Nick says. "A rude awakening came through the fucking door. That's really what happened."

"That his blood or yours?" He looks down at Nick's pants, where there are multiple stains.

"I dunno, bro."

"Well you look a-aight so it must be his."

The security guard had something on his mind. "You let him in?"

"Fuck no bro—she never locked the door," Nick says. He licks his lip.

The friend instantly responds, "That's *exactly* what I'm talking about. It's crazy out here. You can't never take your eye off your back." He shakes his head. "I'm telling you. But hey—where you live anyway—how you getting home?"

"Over by Thousand Oaks park. I'm fine."

"Get yourself a cab, man. You need a few bucks? You never know these days, he could be loading up right now."

"I'll be fine." Nick appreciates the care, but trusts that Phillip won't go grab a gun. During his walk home, though, he looks at each driver coming up behind him. He always wondered why more people don't murder by car.

The walk goes fast and he gets into his apartment. What the fuck just happened? It's back to reality. Nick looks in the bathroom mirror and wipes off the caked blood that's smudged on his lip—he hopes he broke Phillip's nose—might cement his victory. He drops into bed, in hopes of sleeping. Instead he gets a free re-play of the morning's events, courtesy of his brain—how fucking nice of it. Sleep doesn't come. He twitches and rolls around until 11:30—the time he'd normally wake up on a weekend. The crack-of-dawn fight would fit right in with the dreams he's been having, but his body is too sore and his lip too busted to even think it could've been a dream.

He gets his phone and dials home.

"Hi Mom… Good… I've just had a lot going on, that's all… Yeah, everything's okay. I've just been dealing with a lot of stuff lately, that's all… No, it has more to do with that girl I was telling you about. I thought she could just be friends with her ex, since that's what she wanted. But it turns out that he can't handle her being with someone else… Yeah, so I've been thinking about that a lot lately… Yeah, I think he's jealous… No, I don't think he's the violent type—there's no need to worry about that. I just wish I didn't have to deal with it, that's all… Yeah, I'll be fine… Okay… Alright… I love you Mom… Bye."

Nick needs to go somewhere, so he grabs the last of three nickel bags he had bought for ten, locks his door and heads down to the train station to ride to Ronald's apartment. He needs some pizza for his stomach, a blunt for his head, and a friend to get his mind a little bit clearer about what happened and also to get it thinking about something else.

Chapter 31 – Quintavious

Q turns on the radio in the bathroom and hears T-Pain and Plies singing "Shawty." "I exposed her to real, and now she hate lame," he sings along as he gets into the shower. The warm water showers his head and body, and Quint thinks about Ramona. He knows she should be home by now. He's glad she's coming back and can't wait to see her. He shampoos his hair and hears the beat from the radio and starts free-styling over it:

"Long distance love is a bitch for real/

Because I miss you/

Uh/

I wanna kiss you/

Uh/
I'm sick of busting all my nuts into a tissue/
Uh…"

"I don't think your girl kept it as real as you, bruh," Marcus says, and Quint realizes that Marcus is also in the bathroom.

"What are you talking about? And I know you ain't taking a shit in here!" Q says.

"Sorry homie I couldn't wait. But uhhhh, you know Nick at work, right? He told me all about the trip—about Ramona's protest trip. Your girl is a freaky deeky deeky deeky," Marcus says, and then continues telling Q about everything he heard from Nick. All Q says is "Okay" and then jumps out of the shower, gets dressed and leaves the house all in five minutes. He's at Ramona's co-op in fifteen and they're walking to the park in twenty. It's eleven in the morning on a Saturday but with all this crazy news, it feels like the day's half over.

"What's wrong?" Ramona asks as they cross the street. This is the first time they've gone outside when it's been nice out and Q wishes he could appreciate how good Ramona looks in her little tank top, but he just can't.

"I'm good. What's wrong with you?" Quint says with his jaw clenched. He can't stop thinking about all the dudes that know she has a man and were kissing on her and doing god knows what else. They're thinking he's a fucking chump. Fuck that. "I got to stop at a store," he says.

"Okay," she says, looking confused. They walk to the Citgo and the weekend hustle-and-bustle of people surprises Quint—but then again, people always come out when the weather gets nice.

Quint goes back to the beer section and gets a 24-ounce Ice House. Ramona goes to the front and gets some Sun Chips.

Quint sees some old, grungy-looking motherfucker staring at Ramona, and as they're leaving, the guy calls Quint over to him. The man is about fifty years old, and is wearing steel toes and blue jeans so dirty and oily they look brown. "Lemme holler at you, homeboy," he says in slurred words to Quint.

"What's up," Q says, and walks over to the man—they meet in between the pumps and the entrance, and the smell of stale beer is like a force field around the motherfucker.

"Ay, man, I ain't trying to come at you wrong or nothing," the man says, smiling and staring at Ramona, "but I got forty dollars, homeboy, and I ain't had no pussy in a minute, you heard me?"

Q smiles at the man. "Yeah it's all good, OG. What's up?"

"I'm seeing what's up with lil mama?"

"Yeah, yeah, yeah, I'm all about that paper. You wanna fuck her, right?" Q says in the man's ear, still smiling.

The man is swaying back and forth. "Yeah," he says, practically drooling at Ramona, who's still standing about twenty feet away, eating her Sun Chips.

"Yeah, you want to stick it in her, huh?" Q says in a whisper, watching the man's glazed-over eyes stare at her ass while his body rocks side to side.

"Ohh yeah," he says.

"That pussy is good, huh?" Q says, and he sways with the man.

"Yeeeeeaaah," the man says, but before he finishes the word, Quintavious glances around for cops and then pulls a right hook from his hip to the guy's mouth, WHAP!—clocking the man so hard that it sends him spinning into the air and then landing face first, out, on the smooth concrete by pump 2. Quint moves to get the money out of the man's pockets but then decides he could catch him an even worse charge, and that he shouldn't do that in front of Ramona anyway, so he lets the injured man keep his cash.

He turns his head towards Ramona and she looks at him like he's the devil himself. She starts shuffling herself away from him like he's going to attack her. "Wait up!" he says.

She keeps going, looking back at him like he's chasing her. "Who are you?!" she says, slowing but continuing her retreat.

"I can't do it," Quint says, catching up with her. "I thought I could but I can't. I thought it would be cool—you could mess with who you want to mess with and I could mess with who I wanna mess with. But I'm telling you. What I figured out was that I can't look a motherfucker in the eye knowing that he fucked my girl— I just can't do it."

"What? You just assaulted a man. He's unconscious. What are you even talking about?"

"I'm talking about you. I'm talking about all your little free love stuff. I'm talking about you having a orgy on your little field trip." Quint makes sure to keep walking at a fast pace.

"There is a man, lying on the concrete, who might be dead right now, because of you. I am not going to talk about the party during our protest."

"He ain't dead, I just knocked his ass out. He wanted to buy you like you was a ho."

"I don't need you to protect me. I do not belong to you. I am not *your* girl. All this fucking sexist, possessive shit is toxic and I will not put up with it. Get over it," she says, and takes a few steps, then stops, and turns straight at him. "The world is not going to end if I kiss another man!"

A white man runs up to them. "Hey, she doesn't want to talk to you, all right?" he says to Quint. "Leave her alone. I already called the cops and they're on their way."

Quint bites his tongue and holds himself back from socking the cracker in the jaw. He watches as Ramona analyses the situation. "I don't need your help," she says to the man. "He's my friend."

"Friend?..." Q nods his head. "I gotta go." He turns up a side street. "You don't understand the way men think," he yells back at her. "I wish it wasn't true, but it is. You're living in a dream world and I'm not gonna stand around and play into your little fake fantasy. Do me a favor—go fuck as many dudes as you want, suck as many dicks as you want, and do whatever the fuck else you want to do—just don't call me up!"

"Fuck you!" she yells back.

Quint changes directions down a different side street, then a cut, then goes by his homeboy's house. No one's there, so he strips off his sweatshirt and hat and stashes them under a chair on the porch. He's not worried about himself. The only thing he's worried about is the police talking to Ramona. Would she snitch? He knows she wouldn't snitch on him. Would she though? Damn, he doesn't know anything about her. What the fuck is he doing if he's with a girl who might turn him into the police? Is he dating the enemy? He finishes his beer and then stays low on his route back to the house.

Chapter 32 – Nick

Nick's alarm starts beeping. It's eleven thirty in the morning. He hits it off and lies in bed. He could get up but what's the use. He just lies there. Fucking Luana. He needs to just end it. She's too much drama. But then what is he going to do? It's not like there's anyone else. And he really can't even think about anyone else because she's the one he wants. He puts his head into the pillow and tries to think about something else for about forty-five minutes until the phone rings. Yep, it's her.

He answers with a loud "hello," wanting to sound mad. He is mad. He's fucking pissed.

"Hey," she says in a tiny voice so that he can barely hear her.

"So what's the deal?" Nick says. "Did you end it? Make a decision—one way or the other—shit or get off the pot." He's out of bed and walking into the kitchen, his bare feet skidding through the crumbs, dirt, and hair on the linoleum floor.

"I'm just talking everything through with him."

"Talking it through?"

"I've known him a long time and I just feel bad for him."

"Ahhhhh, he's having a tough time?" Nick says, putting on a baby voice. "Poor guy—did you give him a little hand job too? Just to make him feel better?" She's silent, and then he regrets saying it, but then he wonders if maybe she did... Or maybe she fucked him. He has no clue. He doesn't understand her yet. But also she doesn't understand him. Like, how is she not seeing what's going on here? "What if the same thing happened to you? If we were in bed together, right, and then my psycho ex crashes through the door at six in the morning, saying she's in love with me and trying to fight you?"

"I would want to whoop her ass, too." This makes Nick feel good, but he doesn't show it.

"You would want me to go meet her at a bar so we could talk things out?"

"I've always had the belief that the truth will set me free."

"The truth will set you free? Really? Did you believe in the truth when you decided to have me over? And you were still messing around with him? That's the truth? That's just you being honest?" But when the words leave his mouth, he's reminded of what people say to him. People always calling him a fucking liar.

"It's not like you're perfect," she says, barely audible. "I was always taught that guys shouldn't fight in front of girls."

"Wait. Hold on." She's playing games right now. "I didn't leave the fucking door unlocked. How I was raised…" He pauses, trying to think of some shit to say. He scrapes a patch of dried egg yolk back and forth along the counter with his thumb nail. "How I was raised, is that you make the bed that you're gonna sleep in." That didn't come out right. "If you're the one that causes the bullshit to happen, then you're the one that has to sit through it and watch it. That's how I was raised."

Silence. And then she says, "I keep on thinking about…" but her quiet voice trails off into the silence.

"What?" He should just end this whole thing—she's getting on his nerves.

"Nothing," she says.

"You keep on thinking about the fight?"

"No," she says in a mouse voice.

"What then?" What the fuck is she talking about?

"I keep thinking of you inside of me."

"You do?" is all he can squeak out as a wave of desire crashes over him. He takes a deep breath and stretches the back of his head towards his heels, hearing his back crack into relaxation.

"Yeah," she whispers.

"Oh," he says. "What do you got planned for today?"

"Nothing," she says so quietly he can hardly hear her.

"Come over then," he says.

"You can pick me up?"

"I don't have my truck. I'll pay for a taxi though," he says.

"Okay," she says, "I'll see you soon, baby."

"Right on," he says, and hangs up. He looks around his room and notices the pigsty for the first time. He starts picking up the clothes and then decides to smoke a bowl to make the cleanup more enjoyable. After a few hits he sits down and stares at his lighter. It's a generic green see-through one with the two columns where you can see how much lighter fluid you have left. Nick's has about half the fluid left in it. He sits on the bed and tilts the lighter so it's facing the right way and the fluid is equal on both columns. Then he flips the lighter upside down and tries to get the fluid so that both columns have an even amount of fluid. Wow, it's really hard to do. He keeps trying until he hears a knock on his door. He opens it and it's Sly. Sly looks like he's been up all night, but that he's got some energy. Probably high. "What's up man, how's it going?" Nick says.

"Onionhead what's crackin'?" he says.

Nick's been waiting for Sly to come by to help him with the couch. "Actually, bro, help me get this old couch out of here. I have to switch it with the new one I got that I've been airing out for the last few weeks."

"We could do it right now—just drop it off the balcony and then carry the pieces to the dumpster."

"That's what I was thinking," Nick says as he bends down to lace up his sneakers.

"I gotta couple lamp shades I think you'll like," Sly yells from outside on the balcony.

"No, I'm good," Nick says. As he's finishing tying his shoes, he hears a huge smash coming from outside. He doesn't even get up from his crouched position—*I know that motherfucker didn't just drop the good couch off the balcony.* "Hey Sly, I know you didn't just throw the good couch off the edge."

"Didn't you say we were gonna throw it off the balcony?" Sly says. Nick runs over to the balcony and leans over the edge. In the courtyard he sees his nice, clean gold couch laying crippled on the grass—it's frame warped like a parallelogram with the front panel and two out of the four legs laying five feet from the couch.

"I meant that old piece-of-shit couch right there in the main room, not the new one I've been spraying down and airing out for the past three weeks, you fucking jackass. It was already balancing on the railing. Why would I need your help tipping a couch that was already hanging off the edge?" Nick says.

"I was wondering the same thing," says Sly. "My bad, man. Well you might could still use it?"

"Shut up, bro. Just shut up." They both lean over to look at it.

"You right," Sly says, and they both start laughing. "I'll make it up to you. I got some nice lamp shades for you."

"Just help me carry the shit to the dumpster."

As they throw the final pieces into the dumpster, Luana's cab drives up. Oh well, so much for the clean apartment—she doesn't deserve it anyway. He gets his last ten dollars from last night's pants and hands them over to the driver.

"I thought that was the couch you were keeping?" Luana asks.

"It didn't work out," Nick says, looking at Sly.

"Alright then Nick, I'ma bring you some chairs tonight—I know you gonna love these chairs I got."

"Whatever, bro."

Nick and Luana walk up the stairs to his apartment. "Hey," she says, reverting back to her quiet voice.

"I was gonna clean up but I got caught up in something else," he says.

"That's okay," she says, looking down and submissive. Nick lifts her chin up with his fingers and gives her a kiss. His mouth is wet for her. She breathes onto his mouth and then sucks his upper lip. He pulls her little body towards him.

He cuffs the bottom of her shirt and brings the fabric up her stomach, ribs, and over her taut breast. Her body is perfection. How did he get so lucky to be with her? There's a part of him that's always surprised when someone this beautiful wants him—when anybody wants him. Sometimes he's so surprised he's not still a virgin.

They go at it and his mind goes abstract—control flipping between them—submission, dominance, submission.

"Tell me whose pussy this is," she says, rolling in sweat and sucking on his fingers gripped to her mouth.

Dirty talk—not a trick question. It's gotta be hers, right? No, his. His pussy. "My pussy?"

"This is your pussy," she confirms, *whew,* and his penis swells. "Whose dick is this?"

Damn, twenty questions—he wasn't prepared for a quiz.

"Tell me this is my dick, baby," she says.

"This is your dick," he says—and he likes saying that as he gives it to her. Ramona would probably say it was possessive—like she owned his dick and he owned her pussy—and that that is what's wrong with relationships. But fucking is about feeling good, and this feels good. He leans up onto his knees and watches himself fuck her—this is *his* pussy. She spreads her legs wider and dangles her feet in the air. It's like she changes people based on how she is during sex—at one moment being young and shy and submissive and the next being grown up, dominant and controlling. She's every woman in one.

"Put your finger in my butt," she says between moans.

Huh? Do what? He holds her legs as they move together.

"Afraid to get shit on your finger, pretty boy?" she lifts her eyebrows, and there's no way anyone could argue with that. Everything is elevated until her moaning takes a turn.

"Nick! Nick!" she screams, and it's not sex-related.

"What?!"

"There's a roach!" Luana says, shaking him and putting on her pout-face. "Look, over there in the corner. It's running."

Is she serious right now? Nick pulls out, takes a deep breath, and forces himself out of bed and over to get the can of RAID. He bends out the straw on the nozzle so that it's on the narrow-stream setting and creeps up on the insect. When he gets about four feet away, he stops and lifts his weapon in front of him. Ready… aim… fire. He rips him… The roach could run into the closet and have a chance of making it, but instead panics and runs towards the middle of the room. Nick has him locked in, and maintains his thin laser of poison on the roach's body. It is too much for the poor bug, and he flips onto his back— his limbs twitch fast, then slower and slower until they come to a stop—his head cocks to the left and then rests.

Nick tries to get back to business but the smell of roach killer is just too much.

Chapter 33 – Quintavious

Marcus is right, though, if Quint loves her, he should tell her how he feels. He should fight for her. Because when he really thinks about it, he does love her. They have a connection that he ain't never had. She keeps it one hundred and she keeps the conversation fresh—like, he never gets bored around her. And that sex... that sex was off the chain.

It's really time to just put it all on the line and let her know that he's really in this—like for real for real—so he leaves his house.

It's midnight before he makes it over there. The door's not cracked like it normally is so he has to wait for someone with a key.

Luckily a white boy comes up after about ten minutes. "You mind letting me in, bruh? I'm Ramona's nigga. Man. Boyfriend. Partner," Q says, and they both chuckle as they enter.

Quint is sick of fighting—he just wants to be positive; to have fun; to hold her. He passes through the lounge area and sees a pad and a pencil, so he rips off a piece to leave her a note in case she's not there.

As he walks up the steps, he hears something and stops. Hell no. It's a rhythmic sound. And then he hears something else coming from behind Ramona's door. A grunt—and it sounds like Ramona. Plus he hadn't even called beforehand. He walks closer to her room, and hears the thumping noise, wood against a wall. Must be a bed against a wall. He sees the shoes laid out in front of the door and luckily doesn't see any big enough to be dudes' shoes. His chest presses into his neck and the fact that it's a female that she's in there with doesn't make it any better. Motherfuckers who talk about "My girl got a girlfriend" weren't talking about their real girlfriend having a real girlfriend or else they wouldn't say that shit.

He stands on the Namaste welcome mat and wipes his face with the cuff of his jacket. He's sweating so much that the moisture doesn't leave, it just smears across his face. He should just leave. His body is telling him to just leave. Just bounce and ask her about it later. But he doesn't do that anymore. He faces his demons. He faces his feelings. She melted his iceblock heart. No, she helped *him* melt his own iceblock heart, and sometimes he wishes it still was a ice block, 'cause this shit right here is gonna put him to the test. She's testing him. He should be done with her. Why would he play her little game? Should he knock? Yes. No. Yes. He lifts his hand to knock, but his hand deceives him and grabs the door knob and in one quick motion turns the unlocked handle and pushes the door open. Her roommate's empty bed flashes and then there's Ramona, straddling above her reading lamp, balancing on her desk and the frame of her bed. She's swinging a stapler like a hammer into the wall to mount a picture.

Quint exhales.

"What are you doing here?" she says coldly.

"I came by to…" he says, but gets choked up, out of breath, and before he can feel any relief from her not actually fucking somebody, he hits a wall. Why's she gonna talk to him like that? He came all the way over here to make amends and she's gonna be like that? "Never mind, man, I just came to talk things out."

"I'm scared to be around you," she says.

Quint turns towards the door.

"Hold on," she says.

"If you scared of me, I'm out," he says.

"I'm not scared of you," she pauses in thought. "I'm just scared. I don't understand why you didn't just ignore him and walk away."

Images of her with other people swirl around in his head. The dream. The look she gave him. "I think you need to be with someone else. I'm not one of your little hippie friends and I'm not Martin Luther King turning the other cheek and shit. Sorry, when somebody ask me if they could pay me to fuck my girl, I'ma knock they ass out. And another thing—what I heard about you getting all naked with a bunch of dudes on your little field trip?"

"It was a protest. But maybe you don't understand that because you never want to do anything to help anybody else. You only care about yourself."

"So you want me to get on a bus and whip my dick out for a bunch of bitches to help my community? Okay."

Ramona just shakes her head even more. "I can't believe you. 'Whip your dick out for a bunch of bitches.' So your true colors come out. And that's all you think I was doing. You didn't even ask about the actual protest. And since when am I not allowed to take off my clothes in front of other people."

"Naw, you do whatever you wanna do. But I'm out," he pauses. "See, I thought we had something together, but now I see. Like, I was actually looking forward to seeing you, but you wasn't missing me. I'm just some other dude to you. Fuck it. But at least it's clear now."

"That's not at all true. I missed you too."

"Not really. What kind of woman misses somebody and then goes and crushes they manhood like that?"

"I didn't crush your manhood. We were all just having fun."

"You don't understand how dudes think. They see what you did and think you loose and you'll let anyone fuck you. And that your man must be a chump. I'm telling you, that's how dudes think. White, black, hippie, whatever."

"I don't care how dudes think! I'm not gonna react and be re-actionary to the way guys act. I'm not gonna let them dictate how I live my life."

"But you're fucking around and saying two things at once right now. First, you're saying don't get mad at *you* for how *they* act, and then, you're saying don't do anything to *them* when they act out of line, like when dude tried to *buy you* to *fuck you*. You ain't even making sense right now."

"I don't want you to assault people," she says. "Perpetuating violence doesn't help."

He thinks about telling her about his dad and how she don't know nothing about violence and the reason he does the things he does. How he actually doesn't have a problem bringing pain to people—and sometimes it even gives him relief. "Can you stop using some big-ass words?" he says, even though he can tell what she means. "I'm just standing up for what I believe. We not playing Go Fish out here—shit is real. Like, you always talk about changing shit. You think you changing shit by going on a field trip to burn a flag and help some Mexican soldiers? C'mon now. It's Mexicans living in the hood right next to your school. You don't understand. Poverty's not a game. I don't live in the hood because I want to help the poor people or 'keep it real.' Fuck that. I live in the hood 'cause that's what my mama could afford. Soon as I get enough bread, I'ma get my whole family *out* the fucking hood. I don't wanna be living around knocks and niggas getting shot. We didn't live two months without power to help the trees. Fuck that. This just the life I live. You don't understand. Y'all get *stressed out* over some little stuff and just go on vacation—get your mind off it. I ain't been on vacation my whole life."

And this is something he was thinking about last night in bed. "I wish we could run around blowing bubbles for peace, but shit ain't like that out here," he says, and looks at her. "You should be happy. You basically living in heaven. I mean—you rich. You got all the money you need."

"Do you really think that? You really think that because my family had money that my life was like heaven?" she says, her face flush and eyes watery. "My dad was away from home with work stuff most of the time and my mom was too strung out on pills to even be a real parent. Maybe if my parents didn't have so much money then they would've acted like parents. When I had a problem in my life, all I wanted to do was to go to my mom. But as soon as I started talking about anything real, she would ignore me and change the subject.

"From when I was five, they sent me away for the entire summer. And when I got to high school, I was off to boarding school. I haven't lived at home since eighth grade. Not even for summer. And just 'cause I had money you think everything's great." She's trying to hold it together. "What did that money do when I needed a mom or dad to talk to? Money doesn't protect you. Money doesn't stop people from doing things," she says, and she's crying now. He's never seen her cry before. He wants to stop her, to do something to help her. "You don't now what I've been through… what a lot of women have been through… what *nobody* should have to go through… and I had no one to go to." She pauses. "My mom wouldn't talk to me about it," and then closes her eyes, her head quivering. "I had to deal with it all by myself and I couldn't deal with it. I just couldn't... Sorry… I need to be alone."

Quint is silent for a minute. He wants to hold her, but he can't move himself towards her. He does what she asks and leaves. He didn't get to tell her how he feels. His face stiffens and he feels his eyes well up—he doesn't try to blink the tears away because he might never see her again.

Chapter 34 – Marcus

"Ay Marco! Psycho on the phone," Quint calls out to Marcus, who is blasting 2pac on the stereo in his room. He doesn't respond, so Quint has to walk over and bang on his door. "Psycho on the phone for you!"

Marcus opens the door as he raps along to the CD: "Don't give me that 'Buy me this, buy me that' syndrome shit. Bitch, get a job if you wanna be rich." He looks at his brother's hands. "Where the phone?"

"You know where the phone at, nigga."

"It ain't got a cord, nigga, I know that. It ain't 1970."

"You lucky I told you. I was about to just hang it up."

Marcus walks into the kitchen and gets the phone. "What's good?" he says.

"Franky and them niggas wanna get you," Psycho says.

"The fuck you talking 'bout?"

"He said you was the nigga got him jumped on 97th when they got his ass. Talkin' about he was with his baby mama and shit."

"I told that nigga to get the hell on. I ain't set him up. That was Monte and them."

"He say you was the one that started it all, but you was scary to fight."

"Please… I was tryna help that lil nigga out. But it is what it is. We could do this."

"They say the lake. Tonight. But let me tell you something, we ain't taking no chances—they tryna get you and it ain't gon be no one on one."

"I'll box him one on one now," Marcus says, pacing on the linoleum.

"I said it *ain't* gon be no one on one—them niggas is gon be strapped. We gon be strapped. It's on. They been waitin for it to pop off anyway—you just happen to be in the middle, bruh. But ay, I gotta make this money 'for my phone cut off. I get at you in a minute. Matter of fact, I be on the block, so just see me out there."

"Alright, I be out there," Marcus says, and hangs up. He walks back to his room, but stops outside the bathroom to tell Quint what's going down. He tells him the whole story, and Quint just listens, looking serious.

"You're not bringing a piece, though," Quint says. "'Cause when you think about it, if it's one on one, y'all could box, and if it ain't, you don't need to be the one holding."

"You probably right," Marcus says, but is still thinking that he might want to bring one. He walks to his room and lies on the bed. His mind keeps replaying what Psycho told him. He can't rest. He can't think. He decides to get some weed to get his mind somewhere else, so he gets the dollar from his jeans and asks Quint for five more. Quint gives him the money and he heads out.

He walks to the corner and sees Tasha walking with her homegirls across the street. When Tasha sees Marcus, she leaves her friends and comes to him. "I was on my way to your house to check up on you."

"What you want to check up on me for?" Marcus says without looking at her. He can tell that she knows, and he can tell that she can tell that he's not good by the way his eyes are wandering off.

"What you gon do? Lay low for a minute?" she asks.

"Naw I be out there," he says, turning his head, looking at the houses on the left.

"Where you going now?"

"Shit. Bout to smoke. You tryna smoke?"

"Yeah," she says. Marcus can tell she feels for him because usually she's non-stop joking and talking shit.

A little boy rides by on his bike. "Ay lil brah," Marcus yells at him. The boy curves around towards Marcus. "Go pick me up a nick from Teeto house. Meet me outside the store after I get my blunt." Marcus gives the boy the five.

"What you want the green or the hard?" the boy asks as he pedals off.

"Nigga you heard me say I'ma get a blunt, lil jokin-ass nigga, ain't no knocks in my house," Marcus says, and the little boy smiles as he rides off.

Tasha and Marcus walk to the store, buy the Swisher, and then wait outside for a minute before the boy is back. Marcus gives him fifty cents for getting the bag and then the two of them walk back to his crib without talking.

They're the only ones home so they smoke in Marcus's dark room. Tasha tries talking to him but he doesn't give more than one word answers. She stumbles over what to talk about.

"Damn, baby, you got me worrying," she says. And this is the realist he's ever seen Tasha get. He's never seen this deep, pure, sensitive side of Tasha before—and in his serious state of mind it feels good to have her care so much about him—at least somebody does. He feels close to her in a way he never felt before. "Them niggas can take care of all that, you don't have to go," she says.

Marcus doesn't reply. He knows and she knows that he's gonna go. She's just trying to be nice.

The phone rings. They don't answer it.

Then it rings again. They let it go.

It rings a third time.

"Alright I gotta go. You know I gotta do this. At this point, it ain't even up to me." He wishes she would say something because now he feels bad leaving her. He wishes she would yell at him so he could just cuss her ass out and go. All she does is look into his face, raises her chin into her jaw and a tear slips from her eye to her nose to her mouth. He feels empty.

"Make love to me before you go." No, he thinks. This ain't the time to be fucking—he ain't even in the mood. But then again, this might be the last time.

"I don't even know," he says.

"Come here." She pulls his face into hers. He kisses her lips and tastes the salty tears. "Make love to me." She sucks on his lips. He squeezes her into him. This is like his final meal. He reaches down and unsnaps her tight jeans. Her belly relaxes an inch forward. "Baby. Oh my sweet baby," she says. She is the most beautiful, real thing he can think of. He runs his fingers through her hair and grips them together in the back of her head. He lets himself sink into her body. "I want you, baby. I want you now," she says.

"Where's your purse at?"

"I don't want to use one this time, baby. You're too beautiful. You're my love. If something happens I want to have a part of you. Just come to me, baby, let me feel you." His mind is numb. Shit is going down tonight. If he lives, he could end up catching a case by the end of the night. Anything could go down. He needs to just trust her. He ain't in no position to be making decisions like that.

She's breathing, crying and shaking. He shuts his eyes and presses his face against her wet face. This ain't the world I want to bring no child into, Marcus thinks. And it ain't the way neither. But all he does is feel her. He forgets everything for a moment and just feels her. Let this be the way heaven feels if I end up there tonight. "My beautiful man. My beautiful man," she says.

"I love you," he says straight into her ear—not under his breath or because she had said it to him.

"I love you," she says as she cries and moves with him.

Chapter 35 — Marcus

Marcus looks at his face in the mirror of the bathroom and has to look away. "Let's do this," he says, and forces his legs to leave.

Within a minute, he can already see Psycho up ahead a block. And it's like his brain tightens and he can sense everything—the air softly blowing on his skin, the details of every window in every house, every person and car in the street. He passes the newspaper boxes and reads the headline—"President Announces New Threat: Troops move North to Fight Militants."

This is it. Live or die for your hood, right? But Marcus can't help but think of what his dad used to say. That there are two ways of living—one that brings us closer to freedom, and one that just continues the same bullshit we've been living in. Maybe he should say fuck it and go stay with his auntie for a couple days. But naw, he ain't no punk. What would he look like having UNSAFE and UNSCARED on his arms and then pussy out? But at the same time, this ain't really the kind of shit he meant when he got inked up. He meant he wasn't safe in this fucked up world but he wasn't scared of this fucked up world. No, he wasn't scared to *change* this fucked up world.

He walks up to Psycho and says what's up. Quint and the older cats are already up ahead, scoping out the scene. Marcus is ready to get this shit over with.

"Teeto talkin' about meet up by the picnic tables in ten minutes and we'll get the game plan then," Psycho says as he hands Marcus a half-pint of Paul Masson. "Hit this shit my nigga," he says. Marcus takes half the bottle to the neck. "Damn! You lucky you my boy," Psycho says, but Marcus doesn't respond. He's rocking back and forth on his feet, staring beyond Psycho. Time to flip into gladiator mode—it's game time.

"Why you look so serious, my man, you know I got your back!" Psycho says and then kills the rest of the brandy. Before he chucks it to the side, he taps it above his crotch. The glass bottle clinks against the metal of a pistol.

Marcus flashes back to when Psycho actually got his name...

They were fourteen years old coming back from middle school when a high school boy from 115th jacked Psycho for his hat and his jacket.

Psycho, who was Darryl until that day, went home, got his mom's Beretta M9, came back, then found the boy wearing his hat and jacket. Marcus was right there, but there was no way of getting through to Darryl. All he could do was watch. It felt like being invisible, but he still remembers thinking Darryl wasn't really going to do it. Wasn't going to actually go through with it. But then he did.

Darryl shot that boy dead, snatched his Braves hat back off the boy's dead head. He even tried to take his jacket back, but Marcus shoved him until his big eyes registered that Marcus was there and was yelling in his face. He told Darryl the jacket was too bloody and he'd catch a case. So they ran, hopping fences into back yards and dodging dogs until they got to Darryl's house.

The whole thing did earn Darryl some stripes, but Marcus wouldn't have traded all the street cred in the world for what he saw Darryl go through after he shot that boy. Marcus saw him crying. But more than that, he saw him change into somebody different—he stopped telling jokes unless he was roasting somebody—his laugh was different. Even in class he was different. Before, he kind of liked being in class. He would joke around and do his work at the same time. After that, though, he wouldn't do more than two problems on a worksheet without losing his focus and spacing out into his own head. He's been Psycho ever since.

As they near the meeting spot, Marcus squints his eyes to take a closer look because something strange is going on. Who is that? What's going on? It's Franky and his crew from the 100's and they're standing there with Teeto, Quint and the rest of *his* crew— and they aren't fighting! What the fuck?

Psycho had already run up ahead and is now shuffling back to Marcus. "Them Northside niggas started some shit with the whole

Westside, so it ain't no more beef with Franky and them—the Westside coming together against the Northside. Teeto talkin about we got a new enemy so we gon go to the Northside to get them boys tomorrow! Straight up!"

Marcus drops back from the group… *Damn…* He's barely moving forward. He should be happy, but it's almost like his body is dead. He can't feel it. Psycho is ready to fight even though he doesn't even know what the Northside said or did. Marcus hangs his head and shakes it slowly from side to side… He thinks of Tasha…

He thinks of Teeto. About where Teeto will be in a few years. And that's his leader?

Marcus drifts. He knows you have to fight for your hood—but he's also been to school with cats from all over. Everybody has. And ain't nobody in any hood really that different.

He walks past Franky to let it be known that he ain't bitched out. "We good, my nigga," Franky says to him. Marcus nods to show that it's squashed. And now that that's handled, he can't help but really think of Tasha and what the fuck he did. He already knows he's gonna get that call in a couple months and you know she gonna keep it.

Everybody's amped up and excited for the drama; Marcus just feels like leaving. When he turns around to go, a squad car catches his eye. The cop speeds onto the grass and releases a split second siren, and before he even gets out, Marcus already knows who it is. He moves slowly toward him. And it is him. It's him—the purple-lipped cop.

Noooo. Not now… He feels shrunk, like he's the nine year-old all over again; the kid who chased Quint and this cop back to the house; the kid who watched it all.

"Let's go!" the cop yells. "Time to go home!" he says, wagging his night stick like he's herding cattle. "The gangster party's over. You still have time to make it to the belt store on your way home. Let's go. Move it."

It's like Marcus is out of his body looking down on himself. And he sees two Marcuses—one little Marcus and one big Marcus. And there is no time to feel weak because now is the time for big Marcus to fight for little Marcus who didn't deserve none of what happened to him. It's about fighting for Dad, who ain't never coming back. So fuck the cop. Fuck his power. Fuck his little costume—all that don't mean shit. It's now or never.

"Officer," Marcus says, everything inside him bottled like a shook up soda. He forces his limbs to be casual as he walks up to the side of the cop. "Can you explain to me what law we're breaking? Because last time I checked, slavery was over and niggas was allowed to be in the park. So I'm just wondering what law we're breaking."

"This is a known gang area and any gang activity is prohibited. You can go home or you can be cited." And then the cop extends his chin out the smallest amount, trying to place where he recognizes Marcus from.

"Sir, with all due respect, we should be able…" and then Marcus snaps, letting himself explode, his whole body bolting forward, his right fist firing from the hip and smacking purple lips into teeth with the force of ten years' rage. The blow is so lined up, so sudden, that there is no calling for backup on the radio, no grabbing a revolver or a Taser. There is no sound uttered. There is only the uniformed man's head being train-wrecked by a fist, his head leading and his body following directly into the squad car door and then buckling onto the ground. When his head lands on the ground, it is turned off… he's out cold.

Marcus lunges towards him for a follow-up and then stops. He looks around and everyone's looking at him. Even Teeto and the hardest motherfuckers in the hood are frozen—they look at each other and they look at Marcus. There's silence and there's electricity at the same time. A knocked out cop with no backup and no snitching bystanders is uncharted territory. But there's one thing for sure—there's a lot of life sentences in the air for whoever decides to be involved. A few boys turn and cut. "You know they comin'," says another, and then, like a command, the rest flee. All except for Quint and Psycho.

Quint pulls on Marcus's jacket, and the look on Quint's face makes Marcus take a split second to second guess himself. But thoughts are going a million miles per second and there's no time to second guess—*Marcus* has to be the older brother right now—*Marcus* has to take the lead—this is his battle. So he stands back away from Quint, and he looks so deep into his brother's eyes that he is looking beyond.

Then Psycho catches his eye—what's he doing walking up to the unconscious body? He's biting his bottom lip, then lifts the piece from his pants, checks his surroundings, and then leans over the man, index finger squeezing.

"No," Marcus says and puts the back of his hand to Psycho's stomach. "You ain't taking another body. If anyone takes *this* body, it's gon' be me."

"We need to go!" yells Quint. "Darryl! Ay! Let it go," says Quint. He grabs both boys by the cuffs of their jackets and nearly slams their heads together as he brings them close. His teeth are clenched. "We need to cut before the boys get here." He's trying to be the older brother but this ain't his time.

"I'm not leaving," Marcus says. He rips his body out of Quint's grasp and then snatches the pistol from Psycho's hand. These motherfuckers don't understand—he steps back, straddling the cop like he's protecting the body. And then he feels a calm come over him. Complete clarity of thought. "They not coming. He never called. Nobody saw. His radio's right here."

"You gonna end up…" Quint says, and it's almost like he's crying. "You gonna end up just like Dad." And the thought hits Marcus deep inside. What if he will end up like Dad? He wishes he could use the gun to shoot away the thought, the feeling of weakness, of doubt. He steps back from Quint once again.

"I'm not playing. Sometimes you gotta do things you don't wanna do." And now he's really not playing. He's in full control like in one of his lucid dreams; like in control of *everything*.

"Open them back doors. Hurry up!" Marcus says. Psycho jumps in the front and pops the lock on the rear doors. Marcus leans down and scoots his hands underneath the cop's armpits like a forklift. "Get his feet," he says to Quint, but Quint turns. He turns and starts walking away. Starts leaving Marcus and Psycho.

But Marcus ain't gonna fall for that. He's just gonna let him go. Quint is letting him go, and he's letting Quint go. "Get the fuck out of here then!" Marcus says. Quint doesn't turn around. "I'ma meet you at the house… I love you," he adds.

Psycho lifts the cop's legs, and then, with the unconscious head bent in his lap, he slides his ass across the hard plastic of the back seat, tugging the weight of the grown man. He feels around the pockets and holster and removes the 9mm Glock, mace, baton, Taser, and radio. He squeezes the contents of the pockets for keys and then looks up front and realizes the keys are still in the ignition.

"Close the door," Marcus says, and Psycho hinges the man's knees so his feet fold into the car.

"Hold up, bruh," Psycho says. He takes the cuffs out of the leather holster, swings the rings around, wrenches the man's arms to his back and locks his wrists. "Okay, let's be out." Psycho has his eyes on the street a hundred yards away. "Somebody gonna peep this."

"I gotta finish one thing," Marcus says. "Go on. This between me and him." He climbs into the driver's seat. "I'ma see you soon." There's no response. Psycho stands by the back door. Marcus places his left hand on the steering wheel and starts the engine. "I'ma see you soon, bruh! Cut!" And even Psycho wants to stop him, you can tell. Wants to stay with him. But he knows it's no use. He closes the back door without a word.

And then he's out. The gas pedal accelerating him quickly over the grass and onto the asphalt. Psycho fades out of sight as Marcus turns down Patriot and then up Juniper. The whole world is going on around him, but it quickly fades out of existence. No sirens or lights. No speeding. Just driving through town. A box of Marlboro Reds sits in the center console. He tilts the top back and lets the package drag across his wet lip until a cigarette catches. He sparks it and drives; the smoke gathers and swirls slowly inside the windows. He knows what he's doing. He's got two stops to make. Whatever happens in these two stops will determine the rest of his life. But it's good. His mouth creases into a smile because this is it. Why not smile? This is what he's been waiting for. Cruising. On top of the world. He can do whatever he wants—park at that spot by the bottom of the lake and drop the motherfucker in with his feet tied, hands cuffed. Would he sink or float? If he strapped the holster and everything back on him, he for sure would sink. Or maybe he should take him to the old house on some "eye for an eye" shit. *Yeah… This is it. What goes around, comes around.*

Suddenly there's movement in the back seat, but he doesn't look. He doesn't need to. He takes another pull from the cigarette and cruises down the street like he's on patrol.

"To the station…" A mumble comes from the back seat. "Going to the station for back-up." The rear view shows the cop with his eyes still closed, his mangled purple lips twitching and slurring. He's about to wake up. And then what's gonna happen? Do other cops have any idea what's going on? How long does he have before the entire police force has him surrounded? Before Mom is watching him on the evening news? Is that what's gonna happen? Is that how this is all gonna end? Is there only one winner in this world? Do they always win? He never saw himself as one of those crazy motherfuckers that murders people and then shoots himself. But shit, now he sees how it is. The cop dies, and he dies. Prison is death and death is death. Killing the cop is like killing himself. His chest loses its air and feels like a black hole. Naw. This can't be the only way out because that ain't him. He ain't no kamikaze suicide bomber type motherfucker. Naw. He was taught better than that. He's been mentally training his whole life to be better than that. He's a guerilla warrior, sneak-attacker, you-don't-see-me-but-I-see-you, tactical mastermind motherfucker.

A heavy grunt and thump come from the back. "Boy have you lost your mind?" The cop pauses and looks at the door, then at his arms behind his back, and then up at Marcus. Marcus looks through the rearview mirror, through the smoke and the screened partition.

"Yeah," Marcus says and nods his head. "Yeah." He lifts the Glock and sees that it's single action and that the hammer is ready to go.

"You must got a few screws loose, son," he says, still with that just-awake look.

"Call me son *one more time*." Marcus's eyebrows raise and he blinks rapidly, like his eyelids are trying to break his fixed stare.

The cop reviews his surroundings once more.

"I don't understand," he says.

"You don't understand," Marcus says, and nods. "You *don't* understand. And that's the problem." They drive. Marcus watches him in the rearview—watches him trying to bring his elbow up to balance himself along the backseat. He lets the speedometer go up to thirty-five and then five feet in front of the stop sign juts his foot into the brake, the cop's body slamming into hard plastic and then dropping to the floor. "You don't even know who I am," Marcus says. He scrapes the steel tip of the gun across the partition grate as the cop squirms himself back up to a seated position. "And at the same time, I can't shut my eyes without seeing your face. That's the difference between my life and your life…" Marcus pauses and nods his head slowly. "…and that's the problem. That's the reason your life is done."

"I'm sure you have a family that you care about deeply, young man. And you want to see your family. And so you need to pull over and give me back my car."

Marcus sees his father coughing blood, he sees T sitting in jail, and he sees the racist pig in the back seat. He turns on 82nd and slows up to his old crib. "Anything look familiar? Huh? You recognize anything about this street?"

The cop closes his eyes and turns away.

"Huh!? You recognize that gate? You recognize that house?"

The cop faces towards the house, but it's like he's still not seeing.

"Huh?" Marcus says. "Answer, motherfucker. Coward motherfucker—you was a coward when you ordered that shot and you a coward right now."

The cop's mouth opens but there's only silence.

"Why did you kill my dad?" Marcus hears the words whisper of his mouth.

The cop is silent for a moment. "I'm sorry for your loss," he says. "That was an unfortunate situation of self-defense where the suspect…"

Bam! Marcus jams his foot into the brake and the shackled cop's grill smashes into the grill of the partition. "No. Try again. Do it look like there's a jury here? Huh? A judge? It's just me and you. Try again. That was my *dad*." Marcus's voice trails off. The cop slips and struggles to scoot his body from the floor onto the seat.

"He assaulted me." A lump that looks like a tumor has formed on the cop's cheekbone. A solid red stripe connects his left nostril to his mangled lip.

"You tased a little kid over candy!" He wants to drive the car off a cliff. He wants to empty the entire clip into this motherfucker for crushing his life. He wants there to be an explanation but there is no explanation. Even Quint has an explanation—he thinks it's his fault. But there is no explanation. He's right back into his recurring nightmare—the everlasting loop trying to grasp the reason why this happened—there has to be some reason, and if it makes no fucking sense in the real world, then he must be having a bad dream. That it all is a bad dream and when he wakes up it will be okay. But then he wakes up and it's not okay.

And he's here. And he wishes the partition wasn't there so he could just do it. Just end him. He wouldn't feel any type of sorrow if he did.

The cop steadies himself into a sitting position. He forces his tongue into his bottom lip like a chew, and the split purple lip swells and blood stains his teeth. "You ever done something you regret?"

"Shut the fuck up." He should at least just knock him back out—go back there and pistol-whip his sorry ass. "Stop playing games. I know what you're trying to do. But guess what we're about to do? We're gonna take a little ride to 100 Panorama Drive, okay? Let's see, it's six forty-two? They should all be sitting down at that round table y'all got, getting ready to eat. I'll take your wife out first," Marcus's voice is calm and calculated. "Just, you know, so your kids can see how it is to lose a parent. Then I'm gonna murder your kids, and you're gonna see how it is when dads don't have kids and kids don't have dads. Sound good? Let's go. This is justice. Because one little thing you didn't realize, is that niggas is people too."

"If you so much as…" the cop says and then stops himself.

The lawn in front of Marcus's old house has changed, but the chain-linked gate is still there. He's sitting in the very position, maybe even in the same exact car, as the murderers.

"I'm sorry," the cop says. "I really am."

"Shut the fuck up, bruh. Shut your fucking mouth. Now!" And they drive. Up through the north side and into the suburbs.

"I'm not a perfect person," he says, suddenly old and broken. "To be honest, I've been a fuck up my whole life. I was a screw up in school. I screwed up my first marriage, and I've screwed up many times as a cop."

A screw up? A *screw up*? What? Taking someone's life and then nothing happens? Keeps his job, keeps his freedom. Motherfuckers talk about justice. If there's any justice in the world, any sort of consequence and accountability for his actions, then Marcus should shoot this man and ask questions later. And yet here he is, with justice on his side, with more reason than he could imagine to kill this man, and he's feeling some type of way.

Why? Has he been brainwashed to spare this man? To respect his life? Is the whole world brainwashed to love the white man? It ain't some noble shit to let him live—he ain't no better man for doing that. He's a fool for that. Sparing the life of your dad's murderer? "You're going to die too, son," he says. And Marcus can't get himself to challenge it—to call him out for calling him son. He doesn't feel strong anymore. He doesn't feel in control. He feels weak and speechless. "You can take me out, but what's that going to do? I'm a worthless old man. You're the one who's young. You're the one that has your whole life in front of you."

Marcus doesn't like how the cop is changing everything. He liked how it felt before. Not now. Now it feels like the partition is on the cop's side. Like even though he's the one driving, the cop still has the upper hand. You can't win for losing.

"You know how these things play out," the cop continues. "When a cop is murdered, the whole city will be at my funeral." And now it's like he's trying to talk to him man to man, or more like man to child. "You know how it is, you're a smart kid. They increase funding for the police department, and everybody sees you as just another thug."

Just another thug... just another thug... And Marcus is hunched over, hand so limp it slips off the steering wheel. His mind flashes back to when the whole family used to sit at the dinner table. He used to love when Mom did that—said it's family dinner night so you set the table, you bring the food out when it's ready. He would be so excited that he wouldn't even start eating until everyone else was done. His plate would still be full because he would be telling jokes and laughing while everyone else would be eating. Dad would have to remind him. *Hey Arsenio—why don't you take a break and eat some of that food before it goes cold?* A thug? Naw, that ain't him. That ain't never been him, or who he wants to be. He ain't the one trying to bring harm on nobody. He just wants to be safe. Wants people to be safe—where they ain't gotta be scared. He just wants that dinner table feeling back. Why'd they take that away? That one place where he could really be him. Where he felt like he had a spot in the world. Why can't he have no spot in the world? Why is that too much to ask for? Why's he gotta be unsafe, unscared? Why's he gotta be a thug?

He looks at the clock and it's 7:02. The twelve probably on their way now. He can't just give up, just surrender. The countdown is beginning and it's do or die. This is reality. And sometimes you gotta accept reality. If that's how they see him, then that's how it is.

Fuck it.

He can be a thug.

He feels the air reenter his chest. His hand comes back to life and, like a magnet, it finds the siren control on the dash—*Wail, Yelp, High-low.* Yes. He flips on the *High-low* setting and hears the piercing moan blast out of the front bumpers. Drivers part ways and slow to the side. Then he switches it to *Yelp* and the pace of the alarm quickens. Marcus tilts his foot forward on the gas and surges ahead.

"This is a bad idea—I want to help you!" the cop yells over the siren, trying to prop his body up with his elbows. "Help you get out of this alive. Give you a chance before they track our location."

"Give me a chance?" Marcus's back straightens. "It ain't about chance." The speedometer hits 60mph as he speeds up Patriot Boulevard. There's a red light ahead and traffic slows to make way. A PT Cruiser is stuck in Marcus's path, unable to get through the intersection. He swerves right then left to dodge it, fish-tailing for a second before regaining control. "Have you ever heard of a kamikaze?! Them motherfuckers that give up they life to attack some shit?" he asks, keeping eye contact with the cop through the rearview mirror. "Well that's me." He speeds past the sign shop. A little boy riding on the sidewalk hops off his Razor scooter and stares. Marcus slows enough to make a right turn, then resumes his speed. The neighborhoods change quickly.

"You don't want to do this. Listen to me. It's not gonna end good for you."

But Marcus is sick of listening to him. Sick of listening to them. Why does he always have to listen to them? If there is one thing in the world that he is gonna do right now it is NOT listen to him.

"You don't understand—they're tracking us RIGHT NOW," says the cop.

"No. Fuck you! I'm going to *your house*! It's not going to show up."

"Son, why would..." The cop clears his throat to steady his voice, "Why would you want to do that?"

"You forgot? I'm a thug. I'm a wild African thug, running through the jungle spearing motherfuckers—didn't you know that?! Son?" Before the cop responds, Marcus cuts off the siren and coasts down to 30mph. He cruises slowly into the suburbs. Basketball hoops in driveways, rose bushes and flower gardens framing big green lawns. And suddenly Marcus really feels like he's in enemy territory. He feels extra black and like there's a spotlight shining down on him showing the whole world his blackness. Any block now they could come swarming around him. Surrounding him and taking him down like they did Dad. But that ain't gonna happen to him. He ain't gonna let the same shit happen to him that happened to Dad. He's here to get revenge on Dad's life. That's right. Dad is the reason he *has* to do this. And not only Dad, but Mom. And Quint. Fuck it, there ain't no turning back now.

Marcus hits a left on Panorama Drive. He slows up the block. House 42, 46. He keeps driving. 64, 68, 72. They come onto his block. The cop's wife's Chrysler Pacifica sits in the driveway. He always gets chills when he sees the car, the wife, the kids. But every other time he's seen them it's been from inside the bus. Now he's exposed.

The blinds are drawn but you can see the light from inside. Marcus slows to a stop. He stares at the blinds in the window frame. Should he do it? Should he make a statement once and for all that if you murder someone's dad then it's gonna be bloodshed? In the name of justice. Because no matter how they spin it, he'll know and the cop will know what the deal was. That it's gonna be re-percussions and consequences. That he wasn't about to just stand there. That's what he should do. Bust in the door, no ski mask, and mow these motherfuckers down. That's what a thug would do.

He wants what's right. His voice drops to a whisper. "I'm just taking you. That's what I'm going to do." And now his thoughts and his voice are merged. "And just like you, I'm not gonna feel good about it. And just like you, I'ma get over it. And I'ma move on. And just like me, your family ain't never gonna move on. Ain't never gonna get over it." Marcus drives slowly up the block to a ten foot bridge over a little creek bed. There are no houses within view. He pops the locks on the car and gets out. He leads with the pistol as he opens the back door of the car. The cop scoots his body against the far door. Marcus aims at his chest.

The man's breath is loud and tears squeeze through closed eyes. "I'm sorry. I'm no good. You're not a thug."

"Stop talking, motherfucker. You sound like a movie. Stop thinking about what you should say. This ain't a game where you use your police training skills. You hear me? Shut the fuck up. I know what's going on—you're the one that's the heartless thug—I'm just making shit right." Marcus enters the back seat and moves himself up to the cop so his weight is on him. He flips the pistol around and wedges the handle in between the purple lips. "You still wanna talk?" Marcus's face is six inches from the cop's. He grinds the handle of the gun into the cop's jaw every time he utters a sound. "You have something to say? You trying to play me? I'll flip this around, blow your head off, and take out another family member every time you say some shit to try to get out of the situation. It's not about that. Stop thinking. You ready for it? Huh? Feel the life you took away? Feel the life of having to live without your family when it never even had to happen?"

Marcus places his hand on the cop's face and the warm sweat between his fingertips and the cop's swollen skin connects because both of their hearts are pumping and both of their bodies are on high alert and the cells are moving. But sometimes you have to put things out of their misery—lay them down to sleep. Watch them purple lips turn brown. "Do you feel it?" Marcus says, tears in his own face. "Do you feel it?"

"There's," the man pauses. His face wet with sweat mixed with tears. "There's nothing I can say." And the words stick. They stick because finally. Finally he knows. That he did so much damage that there is nothing he can say, nothing he can do to make it better. The man's body goes limp and his head drops to the left and bobs against the hard black plastic seatback. He stays silent.

Marcus grips the handle tightly with two hands as he rotates the barrel into the cop's eye and clutches the trigger. They can lock his body but he's going to stand up for justice. He's a soldier for freedom. He's a freedom fighter. Unsafe, unscared. For Dad. For Quint. Quint… What would he say? And what would Dad say? And Mama? His chin drops to his chest. They would say don't do it. They would say save yourself and live on because we love you. But sometimes you gotta make your own decisions. Stand up on your own two. His trigger finger bends but stops.

There's something inside him that won't let it happen. But what is that? What is telling him not to kill this man? Why is Marcus feeling it when the cop *didn't* feel it before Dad's murder? Should he listen or should he override it? He hates himself if he does and he hates himself if he doesn't.

The Glock gets heavy, and the tip inches down the cop's cheek, lips, and chest, into Marcus's lap. He needs to think, to move, but his body is paralyzed. So he accepts it for what it is. He lets the man live. He uses all his power and moves himself out. Resumes his position in the driver's seat. Turns the key in the ignition. There is no sound coming from either man as Marcus drives and parks back in front of the cop's house.

The cop looks up at him with the eyes of a child. Like a child begging for forgiveness, for acceptance. Marcus stares at him. Their four eyes lock together, millions of light waves darting between their pupils and irises, telling each other stories that haven't been told. He doesn't feel like he made it right. But shit, can you ever make it right? It ain't no bringing Dad back or for sure he would have killed his ass. Naw, he ain't made it right, but he made something right. Deep inside his chest, something cleared up. A blockade like a giant tumor that has been there since the day Dad died is beginning to dissolve, and the stale air trapped at the bottom of his lungs threads its way up, out to the world.

You can create reality. You can change reality. And at this point, you can accept new reality for what it has become. And the cop's spirit is there, and it is real. But Marcus is not a dog that gets swayed by emotion. He is a lion that sees the bigger picture.

"Here's what's gonna happen," Marcus says. And then he goes on. He tells him he's gonna move the radio, the holster, and all that shit in the back seat, and he's gonna move him up to the front seat. That he's gonna uncuff him, give him back his car, and then let him drive off. And that he already knows that he's never gonna hear about none of this shit because no cop, supervisor, or anyone else is ever gonna hear a word about this. And if there's any investigation about what happened today, that he better make up what he needs to make up to make sure everything's right.

The man's quivering face shows that he's got it.

Marcus pops the locks and walks over to open the back door, but suddenly there's a noise from outside the car. A figure flashes out of the house, a white windbreaker, towards him. Marcus lifts the barrel of the gun, shifts his forearms to a propped position over to the hood of the car, and wraps his finger around the trigger. The cop screams. "Noooo Niiiiiiick!" Marcus freezes.

Nick? Nick Nick? What the fuck?

And it is Nick. He's standing still, about to get shot down. And then Nick sees Marcus with the gun out and dives.

What the fuck? This is a bad dream. This is not reality. What is Nick doing here? Crawling in the middle of a lawn? *And me, about to shoot him from the cop car? Did they set me up? Did God set me up?* Marcus lowers the tip of the gun.

Nick's expression is a miniature version of the cop's face as he looks up from the lawn. "Marcus? Dad? What is this?" he says.

There's only fifteen feet between the three of them but Marcus feels like he's in a different realm of reality. Like even if he tried to go up and touch them, he couldn't. It's all fake—the suburban lawns, everything trimmed to perfection, it's all fake.

And Marcus can't do anything but push the words out of his mouth. "I had a talk," he says, but needs to take a breath before he finishes, "with my dad's murderer, Nick."

"Wha? But I was saying that Alex is in the hospital again," Nick says, his eyes open but glazed over. He stares between Marcus and the cop, his father. "What's going on?"

"It's over, though, now. It's over," Marcus says.

A bus rises over the top of the hill and so Marcus has to hurry to follow through with the plan. He uncuffs the cop, transfers his belongings, and lets him out. Nick and his dad watch in silence as he starts to walk towards the bus stop at the end of the block.

Before he arrives, Marcus's footsteps slow and then stop. He turns, deciding that he should be clear about one thing. "And I got twenty killers in the hood with your address and badge number if for some reason it ain't over." Because it's one thing he has learned in life. You can't never put your freedom in another man's hands—especially the police.

-END-

Acknowledgements

Thanks to all the strangers and short-term friends who will never read this page but who taught me more about this crazy world than anyone else. Thank you to my writing teachers Sarah Anne Shope, Cary Groner, and Shirin Yim. Thanks to everyone who proofread and gave feedback on the many drafts. Thank you to my real siblings and chosen ones: Eli, Quince, Piz, Zack, Vel, Tobe, Rel, Alec, Alex, James, Ilesa, and T. Moon. Thank you to all the strong women I've been blessed to learn from—you know who you are. Thank you to my solid parents for your unconditional love throughout this life I chose. Thank you to Lauren, my road dog—once we get this thing calibrated the sky is the limit babe—I love you. Thank you to my kids Izi and Amo, and my godson Kaden. Thank you to my students— past, present, and future—you motivate me and this one is for you. Thanks to Nick Chinlund for pushing this project, and thank you to Yamin Semali for bringing it to life on the audiobook.

Avery Moore grew up in Berkeley in the 80s and 90s. His day job for the past ten years has been teaching in public schools— Georgia, Florida, and now Oakland, CA. He has always been frustrated by the corny or inaccessible books that come out for reluctant readers, so he wrote this one in attempt to change that.

The first draft of UNSAFE UNSCARED was written in 2005, before police shootings went mainstream; since then, Avery has been revising. He likes to think of this as a collaborative project between his 25 year-old self and his 39 year-old self.

Visit UnsafeUnscared.com for questions, comments, inquiries, or links to audiobook and podcast.

♦ ♦ ♦

www.ingramcontent.com/pod-product-compliance
Lightning Source LLC
Chambersburg PA
CBHW050858130726
47900CB00013B/399